Something Different

T. Baggins

Something Different
Copyright © 2011 T. Baggins

First Print Edition, May 2012
Second Print Edition, November 2012

All Rights Reserved.

Cover design by J. David Peterson
Formatted by CyberWitch Press, LLC

This book is licensed for your personal enjoyment only. This book may not be re-sold or given away to other people. If you would like to share this book with another person, please purchase an additional copy for each recipient. If you're reading this book and did not purchase it, or it was not purchased for your use only, then please purchase your own copy. Thank you for respecting the hard work of this author.

Without limiting the rights under copyright reserved above, no part of this publication may be reproduced, stored or introduced into a retrieval system, or transmitted, in any form or by any means (electronic, mechanical, photocopying, recording or otherwise), without prior written permission of both the copyright owner and the above publisher of this book.

Publisher's Note: This book is a work of fiction. People, places, events, and situations are the product of the author's imagination. Any resemblance to actual persons, living or dead, or historical events, is purely coincidental.

Something Different

None of it would have happened if Germanotti hadn't told Michael Maguire he didn't know the meaning of the phrase "fuck it."

"I do know the meaning of that phrase," Michael said, trying not to sound annoyed. What was it about him that made people assume he spent all his spare time cutting the grass, repairing the gutters and waxing the 4x4?

He glanced at the cola he'd nursed for the last half hour. No matter the occasion, Michael was always the designated driver. Always fated to drive loud-mouthed pissheads home while they shouted out his 4x4's windows like football hooligans. Then the next workday, before the staff meeting, they would claim all sorts of outlandish adventures. Michael was honest. He never denied where he went after each Friday night at the corner gastro-pub. He went home, apologizing to Frannie if he stayed out past one o'clock, the limit she had set. After admitting as much, Michael had to endure his colleagues' teasing and listen to their stories:

teenage Lolitas coming on to them in nightclubs, anonymous three-ways with kinky college girls, prostitutes dealing out freebies. It was all pure fantasy. True, Germanotti had talked one of the company's interns into having sex with him in the stockroom. But afterward she'd avoided him altogether, going so far as to take the stairs if Germanotti was in line for the lift. If those were the wages of workplace sin, Michael wanted none of it. If he ever found himself in the market for uncomfortable silences and angry stares, he could always go home.

Now Germanotti gave Michael a moist grin. "I do know the meaning of the phrase," he mimicked. "But I'm Michael Maguire, I have a stick up my ass and a sad little scar where my bollocks used to be, so you'll never hear those words cross my lips."

Michael gave a low chuckle. Germanotti was crude, frequently deluded and terrified of his own wife, whom he pretended to rule with an iron hand. He was constantly on notice for poor work performance and would have been sacked years ago, except Michael kept covering for him. Yet Michael liked Germanotti. For whatever reason, the man was convinced Michael had it in him to someday step out of line.

"I mean really," Germanotti continued, finishing his pint. "Are you so in love with sweet Frannie you've never been tempted? Never wanted to find a little bird and give your cock a go?"

The question was absurd. The answer, of course, was every single day, when he woke up with an erection and headed into the shower to masturbate. Michael couldn't remember the last time he'd had sex with

Frannie, and there were so many rules he was no longer tempted to try. Weeknights were out; she was too tired from housework and spin class and book club and keeping up with her favorite programs on telly. Sundays were a no-go; she tended to go out with friends after church and preferred a nice long evening with the telly when she returned. That left Saturday, and then Michael had to be freshly showered, the kids had to be either asleep or out of the house, and Frannie had to be in the mood. The likelihood of all these factors coming together was about as favorable as a total eclipse. Once Michael had thought that as he grew older, he'd get "past it," as men used to say, and find himself as disinterested as Frannie. But now he was thirty-four and more frustrated than ever. Frannie wouldn't even let him hold her and masturbate, she found the very idea juvenile and borderline deviant. And the kids were always on the computer – the first time he'd downloaded a bit of soft-focus pornography, his son had found it straight away, been blamed by Frannie (Michael still felt guilty about not coming clean) and grounded for a month. So the only safe place for Michael to seek release was in the shower.

As for wanting to "find a little bird" and giving his "cock a go..." Well. Yes and yes. Germanotti was always going on about blondes with large breasts, but Michael didn't even know what his type was. Friendly, nice smile, nice eyes, all those would be good. Surely prostitutes – did they employ that term, or might they consider it offensive? – would be patient and not expect too much ...

Michael and Germanotti lived on the same street.

Parking the 4x4 in front of his house, Michael pulled off his gold wedding band and stuck it in his inner coat pocket. Leaving his titanium-framed specs on the dashboard, he climbed out while Germanotti remained in the passenger seat, confused.

"Michael. What are you doing?"

"You're walking home. I'm walking to Brixton Park."

Germanotti made a choked sound. Then he was grinning from ear to ear. "Friday night in Brixton. My God. I never thought I'd —" He jumped out and hurried up to Michael. "You have money, right? All that rubbish about girls giving it way – don't believe it. They only fuck for cash or drugs."

"I have money." Michael wanted to get away quickly before he lost his nerve.

"Bet you don't have one of these." Germanotti pulled a condom out of his wallet and passed it over. "Shop around. Don't take the first slag you see. I'd come with you, you know I would, but ..." He trailed off, transparently searching for something to say other than the truth, which was there'd be an awful row if he didn't get home.

"I'd rather go alone. See you Monday," Michael said, took a deep breath and started off toward the park.

There were teenagers on the swings, cursing and smoking and passing round a bottle of cider. They shouted things as Michael passed. Still in his usual work attire – suit, tie and polished shoes – he was doubtless overdressed for the occasion. Would he find any prostitutes? Would he look too much like a cop? Suppose he found a woman who claimed to be a prostitute but was actually a police officer? Those consequences were too frightening to even consider ...

No, they aren't, an odd voice inside Michael piped up, rebellious. *So what if Frannie divorces me? It's not as if she enjoys my company, or I enjoy hers. We're only content when we're both quiet and something good's on telly. So what if the kids never speak to me again? They hardly do now, unless they need pocket money. So what if I have to appear in court? It would be the first new, different, unexpected thing that's happened to me in fifteen years ... maybe longer ...*

Beyond the swings were a cricket pitch, water fountains, a public toilet, a small wooded area and a couple of benches. Michael sat down, still nervous, searching for something to concentrate on besides the roiling hope in his stomach ...

A white-haired man stood by the water fountains, talking to a black girl in a spangled hoodie. She didn't look like Michael's notion of a prostitute, which came mostly from *Pretty Woman*. She looked hardly older than his daughter's school friends. She couldn't be out in Brixton Park to sell herself; Michael chided himself for making assumptions based on circumstantial appearances. But when the white-haired man pushed open the men's room door, the girl in the hoodie scooted in ahead of him, smiling and swinging her hips.

"Looking for something?" a voice asked.

Michael looked up to see a boy, no more than twenty-one or twenty-two, smiling at him. The boy had medium-brown hair, wide blue eyes, and very red lips. He looked pale under the park's halogen lights, clad only in a white T-shirt and tight blue jeans. It was late September, not that cold yet, but Michael was comfortable in his suit jacket. A boy in a short-sleeved T-shirt might be cold.

"I'm sorry?" Michael said. The boy was beautiful. There was no other word for it. Why would a young man who looked like that be out in Brixton Park? Surely he was capable of finding a willing girl, surely he didn't have to go out searching for a professional ...

The boy put his cigarette to his lips, took a draw, and smiled. Easing into the bench's empty side, he sat on the armrest, perching as nimbly as a cat. "I thought maybe you were out here looking for something. Maybe it's me."

Michael drew in his breath. Suddenly he understood. "I—" He stopped, gathering his composure. "I - no. I'm not - no."

The boy raised his eyebrows. "You sure about that?" He took another skeptical drag off his cigarette.

"I'm ... I'm heterosexual," Michael said.

The boy grinned. "Are you now? I've heard of het-ro-seck-shulls," he said, imitating Michael's pronunciation perfectly. "Well done. I'm not from around here – I'm from Bethnal Green, if you can believe it – but I wound up here after ... *unfortunate circumstances*. Trying to earn my tube fare back to the city, and no luck yet. Saw you and thought I'd hit a patch of good karma." Leaning forward conspiratorially, he whispered, "I'm popular with the toothless old geezers. It's all good, I suppose, but I'd rather meet up with a real man. Someone no more than ... forty-five?"

"I'm thirty-four," Michael said. He didn't know why the incorrect guess stung him.

"'Course you are. Don't have my contacts in. So what are you looking for? A girl?"

Michael nodded.

"What do you want her to do for you?"

Michael didn't know how to answer. He hadn't thought that far ahead. But the answer – anything – didn't seem particularly dignified.

"The reason I ask is ..." The boy sprang off the bench's armrest and sat beside Michael. "If you want a nice girly shag, wait another half hour or so and a decent femme should happen by. Give it to you just like you get at home, 'cept with extra moaning. But if you want a blow job, best come to me. I'll suck you till you come your brains out and swallow every drop. Takes a man to know how to do it right." The boy grinned again, staring directly into Michael's eyes. "You don't have to go for me, mate. Just my mouth and where it can take you. And it'll be different. Isn't that why you ditched the wife for the night? Try something different?"

Michael looked at his left hand, thinking perhaps he'd left the ring on. But no, it was in his pocket.

"Everything about you screams married," the boy said gently, without censure. "S'all right. Even married men need a good blow job once in awhile. I've always thought the wives should pay me. It's a public service."

Michael started to protest that he hadn't agreed, that

he was a heterosexual man waiting to meet a female prostitute. But then the wind kicked up and the boy shivered, hugging himself as he took a deeper draw on his cigarette.

"So you live in Bethnal Green?" Michael said.

The boy nodded.

"I work not far from there. Take the tube every morning and evening. It'll cost you –" Michael calculated, then named the fare.

The boy nodded. His mouth was gorgeous. What he'd said about it took a man to know how to perform fellatio correctly – maybe it was true. Only twice had Frannie attempted oral sex on Michael. Both momentous occasions had occurred well before he proposed – *before she had me pinned down*, that rebellious voice piped up again. The first time she'd only played around a little, licking and giggling before declaring herself finished. The second time she'd gone all the way, jerking her face away in disgust just before he ejaculated. Allowing his semen into her mouth, much less swallowing it, was out of the question. Frannie said semen smelled bad and tasted worse. Any man who expected his wife to swallow such a repulsive emission was abusive as well as sexist.

"What's your name?" the boy asked, still watching him with those wide, beautiful blue eyes.

"Michael. Michael Maguire."

The boy's eyebrows lifted. He seemed tempted to laugh, but didn't. Putting out a hand, he said, "I'm James Campbell. Pleased to make your acquaintance. Do you have a car around here, Michael?"

Michael shook his head.

"Looks like the men's room still has some action going on," James said, pointing with his dog-end. "Suppose we could break into the ladies' …"

"There's a Holiday Inn just down the high street," Michael said. That far ahead he'd thought, certain he needed a private place for whatever transpired. And if he was going to allow another male to … well, without a doubt, four walls and a locking door would be essential. "We could walk there. Take a room for the night. Unless you have someplace else to be …"

"No. The Holiday Inn sounds like Shang-ra-fucking-la." James leaned close, touching Michael's arm, bringing in his face for a kiss. Shocked, Michael jerked back, more from pure fear and surprise than revulsion. James only smiled.

"Sorry, I forgot. Heterosexual. S'all right, mate, every man likes a good blow job. Close your eyes and imagine a page three girl and you'll have nothing to complain of. Lead the way."

Hotel rooms always felt a little magical to Michael. Anything that took him away from his daily life had a sparkling, supernatural quality he couldn't distill into mere words. And this was a brand-new hotel, with flat screen TVs and streaming video in every unit. They even offered a buffet breakfast each morning. When traveling with Frannie, she always selected tiny bed-

and-breakfasts, where a single bathroom was shared with three other couples and breakfast was determined by the owner.

"This is a palace! Bet it doesn't charge by the hour," James said, throwing himself on the king-sized bed and bouncing happily. "We don't have to leave until – when?"

"Eleven o'clock tomorrow morning." Michael said. Something about James's pleasure in the room delighted him. It was like offering a gift and being rewarded with an unabashedly enthusiastic response.

James laughed. "Don't suppose there's any booze?"

"Probably. In the mini-fridge," Michael said, indicating the small unit near the telly.

"Fancy a drink?"

Michael shook his head. He'd never seen the point of alcohol. All it did was erode control. And the few times he'd imbibed, he'd felt no happier. In fact, he'd felt markedly sadder.

"And I suppose this is a nonsmoking … oh!" James chirped as he discovered the ashtray on one bedside table.

"Thought you might appreciate a smoking room."

James already had a cigarette out. Lighting it, he took a drag and stabbed a finger at Michael.

"Know what? I like you. You're considerate. Polite. There aren't enough considerate, polite people in the world. Believe me."

"You meet a lot of the other kind in … in your chosen pursuit?" Michael asked, uncertain how else to phrase it without giving offense.

James lit up. He was even more beautiful with that

light in his eyes, a sly, coquettish creature with a core of real vulnerability. "In my chosen pursuit," he repeated, choking back a laugh, "I meet the very worst people in the world. And a few of the best. I felt kind of lost, wandering around fucking Brixton Park, wondering how many geezers I'd have to fuck to get back to London. Thought I'd sleep on a bench till the rozzers poked me with their batons. But I met you and I'll sleep here tonight. Can't complain."

"Shall I open it for you?" Michael asked, pointing at the sealed mini-fridge with its pay-as-you-go list attached.

James shook his head. "I don't need a drink to do you, love. I'm ready right now."

Michael went erect. He didn't let himself question the strength of his own response, the throb of need from root to tip. It was like his daily masturbation – possibly wrong, possibly juvenile and borderline deviant, but something he required to keep from going mad. Other men received oral sex, but Frannie refused to administer it. Was it really so wrong to obtain such attention secretly, without harming her? And why not from a beautiful boy? What difference did it make if the mouth was male or female?

James patted the bed. "Lie on your back. Undo your belt. I'll do the rest."

Michael took a deep breath. Removing his suit jacket, he draped it over a chair. Pulling off his shoes, he stretched out beside James, trying to modulate his breathing. "Should we turn out the lights?"

James shook his head. "Watch. You'll enjoy it more if you watch."

Hands trembling, Michael managed to unlatch his belt, unbuttoning his trousers and unzipping his fly. Then James took over, pushing down Michael's shorts and pulling out his fully erect penis. James gave a low whistle.

"This is no cock. This is King Dong," he grinned. "You're gifted, you know that?"

Frannie had always complained Michael was freakish. Michael, sexually inexperienced beyond the hell of his youth, had never been sure. From what little he'd seen of pornography, he considered himself average.

"You don't mind?" Michael whispered. James's hand on his penis was startlingly erotic.

"Mind? I'm impressed." James gave Michael two slow strokes from base to head. Then he parted those red lips and took Michael in his mouth.

The pleasure was indescribable, a warm, wet heat enveloping Michael like nothing before. He felt himself squirt a little pre-ejaculate, felt his anus clench, endured an agonized trembling in his belly as James took every inch of him between his lips, allowing that erect penis to snake down the back of his throat. The mental image was unbearable. Pressing his hand into his mouth, Michael bit into his own flesh to hold back a moan. Then James began to tug with his lips, up and down, up and down, and Michael felt the planet shift, felt the cosmos wheel overhead. Biting his fingers hard, clenching until he tasted blood, Michael ejaculated without a sound, sending a hot gush of semen down the back of James's throat.

"I'm sorry," Michael heard himself say when he

could manage to speak.

James's head came up. He was grinning, licking those red lips like an angel relegated to purely sexual duties. "Why?"

"It was too fast," Michael whispered.

James winked at him. "I'll take that as a compliment, mate. Besides – you're the client. By definition, you can't do wrong."

"I can't?" Michael knew he sounded pathetic, but he had to ask. There'd never been a circumstance in his life where he couldn't be blamed.

James kissed Michael's flaccid organ. Then, crawling up, he kissed Michael's closed lips, looking pleased when the other man offered no resistance.

"You're perfect," James grinned. "I always say that, but in your case, it's true. You're polite, you're generous, and you don't need a freak circus to get off. Call me anytime and I'll come running."

"I ... I enjoyed that," Michael whispered. It didn't seem enough, it didn't seem to capture what he really meant, but it was all he could manage. "What – what do I owe you?"

James sucked in his breath. "Sometimes I hate believing in karma. But I think there's really something to it," he sighed. "Mate. You paid for the room. I had nowhere else to go. You've paid me already."

That struck Michael as wrong. "You need to get home. I'll give you tube fare. It's the least I can do."

"No. The least you can do is nothing. I promise you, I'm correct on that score." James kissed Michael again, unoffended when Michael flinched a little. "Is it too much on your lips? Uncomfortable for a heterosexual?"

Michael didn't know how to answer.

"S'all right. I know what you'd like. Turn over and lie on your stomach."

Michael looked alarmed.

"Not so I can fuck you," James laughed. "Keep your trousers on, mate. Take off your shirt. I just want to rub your shoulders."

Michael did as he was bid. A tiny part of him, almost too miniscule for acknowledgement, was disappointed James only wanted to massage him. But what did such disappointment mean? Was he a latent homosexual? Did he crave anal penetration to fulfill some secret urge?

"You belong to a gym," James said admiringly, running his fingers along Michael's well-muscled arms. "Lift weights? Run?"

"Both."

"Why?"

"Because I need the relief. Besides. Only the strong can defend themselves."

After that, Michael wasn't sure when it happened. At some point he was completely nude, all his clothes wadded up on the floor, James's nearby. Strong fingers dug into his shoulders, pressing, caressing, sending sizzling impulses into Michael's spine. It felt so lovely he wasn't surprised when his long-neglected penis stiffened again. Understandably desperate, it engorged with blood, eager for the attentions it could never receive at home ...

"I like your ass," James murmured.

"Go on," Michael gasped.

"Sure?" There was a rip like a small plastic package opening. "Michael! You're sure?"

"Please." His erection was pressing against his navel, anus trembling. When he felt James's condom-encased penis press between his buttocks, Michael obeyed what he'd read, bearing down as if defecating, not clenching as if maintaining continence ...

A hot iron forced into him, pressing past the ring of muscle and lodging deep within. Michael shuddered, ignoring the pain and overcome with pleasure. He'd never dared put anything into his anus, not even his own forefinger, much less asked Frannie to pleasure him with tongue or toy. But as James thrust, Michael envisioned the other man inside him, bollocks to buttocks, penis buried inside Michael's intestine and head pushed into feces. That image—James withdrawing a brown-stained member—made Michael seize up all over again. This time he bit into his left hand, climaxing after only three hard thrusts.

"You came again?" James asked. He, too, had come, crying out softly.

"A little." There was hot stickiness against Michael's belly. "Felt so good ..."

"Oh, love." James kissed Michael's cheek. "You needed this, didn't you?"

Michael realized he was close to tears. Then they were spilling over, sliding down his cheeks, proving the depth of his satisfaction. Ordinarily shame came naturally to him, but not this time. Tonight Michael felt nothing but gratitude.

"You're perfect," he whispered to James.

James caught Michael's mouth with his, kissing him first with closed lips to closed lips. Michael wasn't good at kissing – he'd hated it as a teenager and fought it as a young man, fleeing to Frannie only to have her tell him he was incapable, inadequate, too slobbery, too intense. So he'd given up, stopped kissing altogether, accepting it was something he couldn't do, like dancing in public or speaking Spanish fluently. But James kept pressing with his tongue until Michael responded, trying his best, using his tongue as he wanted to, hoping it wouldn't be too disgusting. And to Michael's surprise, James slid his arms around him, kissing him back, sucking on his upper lip and joining tongue to tongue.

"I like you," James said again when they pulled apart. "I'll write down my number. Call me anytime, Michael. I mean it. Anytime."

Michael turned up at home around 2 a.m., slipping through the front door and creeping upstairs. Fourteen-year-old Edward and twelve-year-old Vivian were both in their rooms with the lights still on. Michael entered the master bedroom ready for a row, or his and Frannie's version of a row: Frannie enumerating his transgressions, speculating on what others would think of a husband like Michael, and setting down her expectations for the future. Michael tended to go silent. If he felt seriously rebellious, which was rare, he would walk away while pretending not to hear. It was his only viable weapon. Frannie couldn't bear to be ignored.

To his surprise, he found her asleep with her pink

satin mask in place, the telly on and blaring some American crime show. Her prescription *du jour*, a sleeping tablet called Ambien, was on the bedside table along with a glass of water. Michael had wondered why Frannie felt the need for such a drug – he was the one who often couldn't sleep nights – but whatever her friends tried, she tried. Probably she just wanted to sleep on command. Frannie liked things to happen on schedule. Possibly lying down, closing her eyes and waiting to drop off, was just too inefficient.

That night he slept beautifully. When he woke at his usual time, six on the dot, he headed into the shower for his morning ritual. This time it was different. Michael tended to masturbate by either remembering erotic moments from movies or focusing on a specific image, like a page-three girl's perfect breasts. He never inserted himself into his own fantasies – nothing could make him lose an erection faster than self-awareness. He was always someone else, Brad Pitt atop Angelina Jolie, perhaps, but never Michael Maguire. This time, though, he started by thinking of James's face and ended up replaying that moment he'd felt James's penis stabbing between his buttocks, knowing he was about to be penetrated and wanting it desperately. That made Michael ejaculate so hard he somehow managed to spray semen all over Frannie's rack of scented shower gels. Part of him was tempted to leave it that way, to let her find the bottles contaminated and – knowing Frannie – throw every last one in the rubbish bin. But he had to pick his battles. Besides, it was almost more amusing to rinse off the bottles – not too well – and let them dry with a faint, mysterious glaze. The next time

Frannie lathered up, she'd be giving herself a very different skin treatment ...

He thought of James all day long. Around half-ten he was tempted to go round to the Holiday Inn and see if the young man had checked out yet. But Frannie needed his help with the grocery shopping, then she wanted the guest bathroom toilet repaired – every time his son's friends used it, one of them managed to clog up its innards. Michael liked working with his hands and was a decent amateur plumber, mechanic and electrician. He'd written textbooks on all three subjects, and in the course of his research he'd learned all the basics. He'd even selected the photos himself and helped the art department with the layout. Germanotti, in charge of keeping the division's science textbooks updated, often accused Michael of being a control freak when it came to his books.

"You need to take that energy and put it into a novel," Germanotti liked to say. Of course he'd been writing his own novel for the last five years, to hear him tell it, and Michael had yet to see any evidence this towering work actually existed. Not that he was any better. He hadn't successfully written a piece of fiction in fourteen years – almost as long as he'd been married to Frannie. But Michael didn't blame her for that. She didn't give a damn about his writing one way or another, and never interfered when he went up to his office to draft a new textbook. The problem was inside Michael. He couldn't name it, couldn't define it, but he knew it arose from within.

By eight o'clock, he was so keyed up by thoughts of James, he decided to try something unprecedented. He begged Frannie for sex.

He started with a shower – just a shower – and dried his hair and moustache carefully, since she didn't like being nuzzled with damp hair. His roots were showing. He'd have to recolor tomorrow. Otherwise he looked presentable, surely. He was the fittest husband on the block, better built than even the twenty-somethings, and he knew Frannie liked that. She enjoyed listening to her friends complain about their husbands' pot bellies and love handles and then casually mention that Michael could still get into his wedding clothes.

"Please. I'm just so aroused," he told her, pretending not to notice her frown. "I want to make love with you. Please, Frannie. Please."

"Oh, for God's sake. Fine. As soon as this program is over."

She needed a lot of foreplay, which didn't bother Michael at all. Frannie was still quite pretty, with frosted blonde hair, sharp eyes and a cheerleader's smile. She'd thickened just a little after two children, which didn't matter to him, but she was always going on about it, always threatening to have liposuction. Tonight she let him use his mouth on her breasts and even her clitoris. He kept going, hoping to do the impossible and trigger an orgasm, until her hand touched him on the head and she said in a perfectly cool voice, "All right. I'm ready."

"Will you turn over?"

"Oh, Michael," she sighed, as if he asked her to pop round next door and invite their neighbors for group sex. "Can't we just do it normal?"

So they did, and even with his eyes open and

Frannie beneath him, Michael had no trouble imagining he was inside James. He could see him, smell him, hear the sound of his voice. If he hadn't been accustomed to biting on his hand before climax – a very old habit and one Frannie actually approved of – Michael would have cried out James's name as he let go.

Afterward she turned on the telly. "Did you …?" he asked.

"Of course."

She always said that and he never believed her. During their brief courtship she'd always faked a climax and he'd been too inexperienced and infatuated to know the difference. Then two years into their marriage, she confessed she'd only actually had one or two orgasms in her life and would no longer "put on a show" for his ego. That made Michael angry, so angry he had to separate himself from Frannie for a couple of days, during which time he'd been incommunicado at a hotel and she thought he'd left her. Michael knew he wasn't much a person, that when it came to character attributes he was deficient in every way, but he had never, never asked anyone to lie to safeguard his self-esteem. He could bear up to all the truth the world could throw at him.

And he should have divorced Frannie then, he knew that now, but it hadn't been so simple. Edward had been a toddler and Vivian was on the way. Besides, Frannie had been genuinely contrite and done her best to make it up to him. By then he knew she'd married him for his money, no great sum but enough to assure a very comfortable middle-class life. For someone like Frannie, who'd grown up in council flats dreaming of a detached house in the suburbs, Michael had been a winning lottery ticket. And he, in need of someone, had chosen Frannie on the same sort of whim that made him choose James.

Frannie fell asleep on schedule, thanks to Ambien, but Michael was awake far into the night. He had every intention of seeing James again. Perhaps he was a latent homosexual – that didn't matter to him, he'd never looked down on anyone for his or her sexuality or considered homosexual intercourse morally wrong. He *did* consider infidelity morally wrong, but what was Germanotti always saying? "It is what it is." Generally Michael hated that phrase, thought it was too often used as an excuse for inaction, but in this case it applied perfectly. He had met someone special and had to see him again …

The only good thing that came out of his most recent fatal fucking attraction, James Campbell told himself, was hooking up with a new regular in the suburban purgatory of Brixton Park. He often had bad luck in parks. Twice he'd been forced – not raped, not in the classic sense, but injured by men who went too far, then didn't even bother to pay him. Or his evening was devoured by timewasters, curious tossers without a fiver to their name, hoping the first time would be free. James, who hated sex as much at twenty-one as he had at twelve, never gave away so much as a kiss for free. Everyone had to pay. There was nothing in the rule of karma against charging a fair price.

But Michael Maguire was the sort of miserable, self-repressed, half-dead-in-the-harness type who kept rent boys like James alive. That evening in the Holiday Inn had been sweet. Michael was clean, polite and easy to please, utterly clueless that James faked his own orgasm after their two-minute fuck. What did Michael care? He'd gotten a blow job and a dick up his ass and seemed pretty goddamn pleased with both. Besides, James never faked it maliciously. It was just hard for him to get off, fiendishly hard, and with a new client pretty much impossible. But that was the magic of condoms. All he had to do was put on a good show with his face, moan convincingly, and pull off the condom. Not one man in a hundred would ask to see the evidence. So while the client stretched and moaned and pulled his shit together, James tossed the rubber in the toilet and flushed. Happy endings all 'round.

After Michael left, James had padded around the hotel, filled up his ice bucket for no reason, watched cable TV and talked himself out of raiding the mini-fridge. Poor Michael, so innocent in the ways of the world, had given Holiday Inn his credit card imprint and then left James behind to do anything in the room, including drink every overpriced miniature bottle of booze and watch ten hours of premium porn. But James had done none of it. Of course, karma or no karma, James probably would have yielded to temptation if Michael had been an asshole or a cheapskate. But Michael had been ridiculously generous, ludicrously inexperienced, and James had to look at his face in the mirror each morning. So he drank none of the booze and ordered none of the porn. He considered the missed opportunity an investment. Michael would look at his credit card statement, realize belatedly what could have happened, and be all the more eager for repeat engagements.

As for Mr. Fatal Attraction, James tried not to think about him. God knew it wasn't about sex. They'd never done it, not once. Kevin was involved with another man, but he'd toyed with James emotionally for more than a year now. James had followed Kevin out to the suburbs thinking this was it, the day had come, Kevin was finally leaving his cunt of a boyfriend and striking out in search of real love. James was certain with the right person he could feel something, get off effortlessly, have the sort of roses-and-chocolates sex life the rest of the bleeding world enjoyed. And James looked up to Kevin, worshipped him, adored the way he spoke, the way he shot pool, the way he lifted a pint. Kevin was everything a man should be and everything James wanted. But when he got to the suburbs, Kevin and Cunt-Boyfriend had patched things up. James, who'd rushed out impulsively, was left in 4x4 hell with no cash and no way home.

And then along came Michael, paying too much, expecting too little, moved to tears by a little TLC. James smiled at the memory, but not unkindly. Moments like that actually made him feel better about – well, almost everything.

They were supposed to meet at an old hotel called the Nautilus. James had imagined a sort of fitness club with rooms to let, like the old-style YMCA, but after asking around, he was directed three times to a hotel with a seashell over the door.

"This the Nautilus, mate?" James asked the doorman.

The doorman jerked a thumb up at the awning flapping overhead. "What d'ya think?"

"Don't have my contacts in. Bet it says Nautilus. Cheers," James said, striding into the lobby with a spring in his step. Confidence, it was all about confidence, coupled with a sweet smile. Put the two together and most of the time, no one would stop you.

Michael was sitting in the bar. This time he was dressed more casually – sport jacket, polo shirt and khaki trousers. Why did he wear that moustache and that old-man haircut? No wonder James had guessed Michael's age incorrectly. There was an attractive man in there somewhere, beneath the hair and the dad clothes and round specs. He needed to be taken down to studs and refurbished, that was all.

"Aren't you a sight for sore eyes," James said, turning on the smile at full wattage. He saw the response in Michael's eyes and took his time climbing onto the barstool, spreading his legs a bit so Michael could get a good look at his package. "I like the specs," he lied.

"Meant to take them off before you got in," Michael said.

"Ah, yes, well, I'm early," James admitted. He'd ducked out of the flat ahead of schedule due to an unexpected appearance by his landlady. "Eager to get here. Make sure you didn't stand me up."

Michael smiled slightly, looking at the tops of his

loafers. "You don't have to try and flatter me."

James never wavered when someone called him on his bullshit. He just kept smiling and lying until the topic changed or his accuser ran out of steam. "Why would you say that? Because I like your specs? Or because I turned up early for you?"

Michael studied James's face. Then he pointed at the small drink menu. "It's happy hour. Shall I get you a drink?"

"I never drink when I'm working. What's in that?" James pointed at Michael's glass.

"Cola. I never drink at all."

"A sober man keeps it up longer." James leaned close to Michael, pitching his voice low. "I'll bet you and wifey had one hell of a romp last weekend, am I right?"

Michael gave him that same slight smile. "Well – for us. Yes, we did."

James wagged a finger. "Even heterosexuals enjoy expanded horizons."

"I'd like to expand them further."

Oh, yes. He's gagging for it, James thought. With any luck that meant James would enjoy another luxurious night on a hotel mattress instead of creeping back to his futon at 4 a.m.

James touched Michael's knee lightly, casually enough to keep from drawing attention. "So let's go upstairs."

T. Baggins

The room was nice for an old hotel, which was to say substandard compared to Brixton's brand-new Holiday Inn. The bed was only a full, the carpet was patched, there was no mini-fridge and satellite telly cost extra. The room had been retrofitted with a toilet and sink, at least, but the shower was down the hall.

James limited himself to one quick glance around. Staying focused on the client was essential. So the moment the door closed, James pushed himself into Michael's arms, lifting his face eagerly.

"Since last week, all I've thought about is you. That huge cock, I have to see it again," James said with the usual simulated breathlessness. At least in Michael's case, the reference to a huge cock was literally true. "This time I want you in me. I need you, I need you so bad, I—"

Michael's hand moved up. Gently, he slipped two fingers over James's lips, pressing them down and holding. He kissed James's forehead. "May I undress you?"

Thrown off his game – no one had silenced him in mid-patter before – James nodded. Letting himself go loose-limbed, he didn't resist as Michael removed his mac. Underneath he wore a short-sleeved T-shirt; Michael pulled it off, mussing James's hair and carefully stroking it back into place. James hoped he should be flattered by Michael's stare. It was intense, devouring, almost intimidating.

The hotel room was chilly. James's nipples stiffened into hard pink nubs as Michael continued removing his clothes. Michael undid James's belt and unbuttoned his fly, working the tight blue jeans down until James obligingly lifted one foot, then the other. Once the pants were off, James had a feeling such a methodical man would remove his socks before heading up to the main event, and he wasn't wrong. Michael freed James of each sock before gently pushing down his shorts. Michael's hands were trembling, that cannibal stare now locked on James's semi-erect cock.

"Touch it," James said.

Michael hesitated. His breath sped up. He wanted to. He really wanted to.

James took Michael's long-fingered hand and closed it around his cock. "See? Easy. So what'll it be tonight? What do you want?"

"I want to fellate you."

"Steady on! You want to fillet me?" James gave an incredulous laugh. He knew better than that – clients as green as Michael couldn't stand to be laughed at. But fortunately Michael didn't seem offended.

"I want to, um, perform oral sex on you."

"All right." James tried not to look as dismayed as he felt. The odds were slim that he'd be able to come, and not coming could be disastrous. Best to put Michael off the notion, quick.

"Mind you, all my condoms are spermicidal. Little tart on the tongue. But you know the drill, safer sex and all that …"

Michael shook his head. "No condom." He spoke

like a man who'd been fantasizing about this particular act for days.

"No? Very well, then. Cheers." Grinning as if delighted, James sat on an armchair as Michael knelt before him. James wished he had a secret weapon – porn on the telly or a butt plug – but no. He'd just have to imagine something sexy. A BMW or a Mercedes, maybe ...

Michael kissed the head of James's cock. The kiss was long, wet, vibrating with suppressed desire. Then his tongue began working down in hot, precise circles. Eyes open, unhurried, he licked every millimeter, holding James's cock steady as he stroked the base with his thumb. Then Michael took James entirely in his mouth, squeezing his lips around the root, sliding up and down. It was the best beginner suck-off James had ever had. He found himself grinning, digging his fingers into Michael's hair and pushing his head up and down. Dribbling a little pre-cum as he focused completely on the sensation, James felt his asshole clench and thought maybe, maybe ...

But then he heard Michael's belt unfasten. Heard his trousers unzip. Those two unmistakable sounds threw everything around James into sharp relief. He was in a strange room with a man he didn't know getting fucked because it was all he was good for. The possibility of orgasm popped like a soap bubble.

Michael, at least, was getting there, giving himself a proper wank with James's cock still in his mouth, softening as it moved in and out between his lips. At the last moment Michael released James's cock, made a choked noise and shot a white jet against James's inner thigh.

"You ... you didn't ... like it," Michael gasped, still shaking with his own climax, barely able to speak. His eyes were open and focused on James's cock, red and limp and gleaming with spit.

James didn't know what to say. Kevin and Cunt-Boyfriend were back together. He owed his landlady two months' rent. His telly was on the fritz and it seemed like no matter how many men he fucked, there was never enough money to get ahead and put a little by. James wouldn't be pretty enough to do this forever. Where would he be in ten years? In twenty? For a second he felt like he would cry.

"Earlier. You put your fingers over my lips. Why?"

"Because you were lying." Michael tucked himself back into his shorts, zipping up his trousers and fastening his belt. "I don't need that."

"Most people love it."

"I don't. It's distracting." Michael nodded toward James's limp cock. "Why didn't you enjoy the fellatio? What did I do wrong?" He didn't sound angry.

James felt close to tears again. If he said the wrong thing, his bi-curious suburban family man would bugger off and find a nice cheery rent boy without any issues. And James was sure to say the wrong thing, because everything he touched turned to shit these days.

"You didn't do anything wrong. It felt good. Maybe go a little faster next time, but otherwise – good. I just ..." James drew a deep breath. "It's hard for me to come with men I don't know. I have to get used to a client first."

"So last time. I thought you climaxed. You

pretended?"

James sighed again. "Men pay me to make them feel good. And not just physically. If they realize I don't like it as much as they do, I'll get knocked about. Put in hospital or worse."

"But it makes no sense." Michael seemed to be speaking to himself as much as James. Rising from the floor, he shifted to the bed. "I mean, I can pay you to take your clothes off. To touch me. To let me touch you. But I can't expect you to have an orgasm on command, no matter how much money I give you. And the fact that you won't, even though it would be easier, even though it would be safer …"

Michael lifted his head. He looked James in the eye, as if forcing himself to admit something ugly, something difficult. "I think it means you won't sell out. Not all the way. There's a part of you no one can buy. Not with money. Not even with violence."

James had no idea what Michael was talking about. Sitting down beside him, he placed a hand on the other man's arm. They made an odd pair in the room's framed mirror, Michael fully dressed and James completely nude.

"Believe me, I sold out all the way a long time ago," James said. "But the fact that you get why I can't just …" he snapped his fingers, jealous of the ease with which other males shot off. "It means a lot. I like you, Michael."

Michael's eyes locked with his, light green and acute.

James didn't flinch. "Do you like me?"

"Too much."

"No such thing," James said with a saucy little

wiggle. Inside he thought, *give it three weeks and he'll never want to see me again.*

The next week they met at the Nautilus again. Not wanting to scare Michael, James had phoned to outline his plan in advance. As expected, Michael had reacted uncertainly.

"What if I ... suppose I ... get an erection?"

James fought back a laugh. There was something endearing about the way Michael used the correct terminology for everything. "Deepak is a professional. A licensed masseur. He doesn't pay any attention to male blood flow below the waist," James said, leaving out the fact Deepak earned far more cash as a rent boy than as an itinerant masseur. "He'll bring over his massage table, loosen you up, and then we'll fuck till you collapse."

"Will you have a massage, too?" Michael asked.

James was startled. Twice a week he popped in to see his mum. Once a month he saw his dad. His best friend Marla was busy ever since she'd squeezed out twins, but they met up whenever they could. But out of all the people James supposedly held near and dear, his client Michael was the only one who seemed to truly care if James was properly taken care of.

"Let me get you breakfast," Michael had said the morning after their last meet-up. Considering the fact

James hadn't managed to get off and Michael had been forced to service himself, James should have been nursing two black eyes and a bruised ass. Instead he was being invited to breakfast by a man so polite, he wouldn't even use the phrase "let me buy you." And now upon hearing that he, Michael Maguire, the world's tensest human being, was going to receive a professional-quality massage, Michael's first thought was to wonder if James would receive one, too.

"Deepak will massage me if I want," James assured Michael. "But I like watching the action unfold. If he does a good job and you enjoy it, that's enough for me."

Michael paced like a caged lion while Deepak put on his music, lit his aromatherapy candles and set up the massage table. Then Michael undressed with jerky mechanical movements, taking refuge beneath the white sheet and lying on his belly. James found the whole run-up amusing in ways he couldn't explain. Michael shuddered when Deepak's big, strong hands dug into the knotted muscles around his neck and shoulders. But he gradually relaxed, eyes closing, no longer trembling with resistance. Smiling, James began to undress.

He wasn't shy of Deepak. They'd fucked once or twice, enough to know they weren't into each other. James wasn't stripping to entice Deepak, young and handsome though the other man might be. James was stripping because he knew Michael loved to look at him. So he wanted to be bare at the right moment, pale skin, pink nipples, red lips and red cock, to add to Michael's pleasure however he could.

"Why don't you ever moan?" James murmured in

Michael's ear as Deepak kneaded his shoulders.

"Kids'll hear," Michael muttered.

"Your kids know what you and wifey are up to. But why don't you moan here? When you're with me?" James persisted.

Michael didn't answer.

"You can moan when you're with me," James whispered, kissing Michael's ear.

"Turn over," Deepak said, lifting the sheet.

Slowly, reluctantly, Michael did. His cock was fully engorged. Deepak dropped the sheet below it and began to stroke Michael's hard belly with both hands. Michael's cock trembled, balls stiffening. Deepak's stroking wasn't quite massage-school technique, James knew. This particular caress came from the rent boy playbook.

"I wish you'd let Deepak get you off," James said, lips brushing Michael's ear.

"I want you. I trust you," Michael gasped, looking at him. It was true. Something in the other man was afraid of being jerked off by a stranger, though James couldn't imagine why.

"He won't touch you if you don't want it," James said, shooting Deepak a glance to make sure they were on the same page. "I thought this would be fun for you. Something different. And I'd enjoy watching you lose control."

"You would?" Michael came out of himself for an instant, focusing completely on James. And James felt his cock dribble in response, aching for the release he found so difficult to accept.

"I want to see you spurt. Hear you moan," James

said. Fastening his mouth on Michael's ear, he began kissing and tugging with his teeth even as his right hand seized his own cock. Deepak had Michael in both hands, working him brutally, pulling mercilessly. Michael's breath came faster, turning into gasps, and when he tried to stifle himself with a hand he couldn't bear it. Fascinated by the sight, James's own hand pulled frantically, squeezing, hurting, feeling too good for words. Michael's eyes opened suddenly, locking on James's, and it made all the difference for both of them.

"Next time you'll fuck me," James said. "You'll fuck me so hard, I'll shit myself because I can't hold it in. Because you're too much for me ..."

"Oh God," Michael cried, pumping like a volcano.

"Michael," James whispered, squirting onto the carpet. Making the other man come with dirty talk was easy. More problematic was how much James wanted everything he imagined to be true, at least in this moment.

Deceiving Frannie was unexpectedly simple. Since embarking on her romance with Ambien, she never noticed if Michael got in late on Friday nights. But after his third "adventure," as he thought of each occasion, Michael decided it was too hard, rushing back to the suburb lightheaded – not to mention sore-cocked – just to please a snoring wife. There had to be a better way. A way that wouldn't cause Frannie or the kids undue anxiety while allowing Michael more time with James.

James didn't think much of the Nautilus, so for their fourth encounter Michael booked a room at the Hilton in Green Park. He rang up James to deliver the news. To Michael's great satisfaction, James let out a happy squeak. Reeling off the amenities in a deadpan voice, Michael imagined James's expression.

"Twenty-four hour room service ... state-of-the-art climate control in all rooms ... bathrobe and slippers ..."

"Where have you been all my life?" James sounded incredulous.

Michael tried not to take James's delight too personally. God only knew where the young man lived or how he kept things together from day to day. Half of Michael insisted James's personal life wasn't his problem. Theirs was a simple transaction, old as the human tribe. But Michael's other half, the researcher and author of textbooks, saw no harm in learning more about James. Knowledge, like truth, could never be a bad thing. Michael believed that completely, even when his belief led to pain. And knowing more about his employee might even make their adventures more satisfying, if he could get up the courage to ask.

"So what do you want tonight?" James asked.

They still had their clothes on. Michael was in an armchair. James was on his lap, arms around Michael's neck, jeans-encased buttocks rubbing along a strengthening erection.

"Intercourse."

James made a show of pretending to misunderstand. "Right-o. Me inside you," he said, even as he pressed harder with his rear – up, down, and up again.

"Me penetrating you." Michael kissed James slowly, tracing his bottom lip. He had grown more comfortable with kissing. Apparently it wasn't about technical perfection, like an Olympic gymnast's parallel bar routine. It was about warmth, wetness, closeness.

"Fine." James pushed down his jeans. Tonight he was commando beneath them, all erect penis and bare buttocks. He started unfastening Michael's belt.

"Not here."

"What do you mean?"

"Not in this position. Woman on top. I don't like it."

"Pardon me, mate, I'm no woman." Gripping his penis, James waggled it at Michael.

"Sorry. Partner on top," Michael said hastily, embarrassed by his slip. "Can we move to the bed?"

"Oh, we can do whatever you like, love." James flashed his high-wattage smile. Michael hated when James quoted from the Book of Rent Boy, but he did adore that smile. Even when it was patently false, inspired by free cable and a breakfast buffet, something inside Michael lit up in response.

Tonight Michael had brought his own condoms, an American brand that would actually fit him, not go on like a tourniquet. He'd purchased extra lubricant, too, which he spread atop the condom. Stomach clenching excitedly, he straightened when he was ready, on his knees with his penis in hand. James shifted onto his elbows, buttocks raised.

"Go on," James encouraged over his shoulder.

"Don't make me beg."

Slipping two fingers between the other man's buttocks, Michael found James's anus and began stroking it gently. As Michael imagined, it was exactly the same color as James's penis. Somehow that confirmation was so erotic, Michael felt his own member jerk, pre-ejaculate forming on the head. For the last few days all he'd fantasized about was penetrating James, holding him from behind and thrusting for hours, for days. Trying to slow his breathing, Michael did his best to enter the other man's rectum with great restraint, going extra slow as James shook with suppressed pain. But when Michael looked down and saw his penis half-buried – when he heard James gasp, saw those white buttocks clench – he couldn't hold back.

"I'm sorry," Michael panted as the semen shot out in a humiliating rush. "Sorry. Sorry."

He stripped off the condom. Crossing the room to the bathroom – *en suite*, this was a Hilton after all – he flushed the prophylactic away. Then he soaked a flannel in warm water, added soap and brought it back to James, along with a dry towel.

"What are you – oh." Catching his breath, James smiled as Michael slipped the moist flannel between his buttocks.

"I know it only took me thirty seconds," Michael said stiffly, still embarrassed, "but I made a bit of a mess." As he spoke he shifted to the dry towel, kissing James on one round, firm cheek. Then Michael returned to the sink, washed his penis, scrubbed his hands, and dried himself thoroughly. When he returned to the bed, he found James nude and lighting a cigarette.

"Take off the rest of your clothes," James said, pulling back the covers. "Get in with me."

Michael obeyed. He got under the soft white sheets. It felt good when James slid his arms around him.

"You liked fucking my ass."

Michael nodded.

"The more you like something, the harder it hits you. You'll last longer next time."

"But I don't want this to just be about me." Michael knew the statement was absurd but he couldn't keep it in. "I want you to feel something, too. Even if you can't have an orgasm, I want to please you."

"I know, love. You're generous. It's one of the things I like about you." James's fingers moved lightly through Michael's hair. "Can I ask you something?"

"Yes."

"The hair around your cock is ginger. Your roots are ginger. Why do you dye your hair and moustache brown?"

"Because ginger hair on a man isn't masculine."

James snorted. "Says who?"

"Everyone. I was teased from my first day in school till I graduated. It was like walking around with a bullseye painted on my back."

"Excuse me. Ron fucking Weasley is a ginger."

"Who's that?"

"Oi!" James's eyes narrowed. "Pull the other one, mate!"

Michael laughed. He didn't laugh very often. The sound was almost inaudible. "I know. Ron Weasley is Harry Potter's friend. My Viv's read every last one of those books. Seen all the movies, too."

"Bet she has." James resumed stroking Michael's hair. "Love your kids?"

"Hardly know them anymore. Maybe it's my fault," Michael sighed. "Maybe I spend too much time in my own head."

"Love wifey?"

"No."

James seemed unprepared for that. After a moment he said, "Well, maybe it's time to upend the apple cart at home. Let her see you as a ginger. That might get things sizzling in the bedroom."

"I doubt it. Frannie's the one who started me coloring my hair."

James goggled at Michael. "Why?"

"I told you. Ginger hair isn't masculine. She hates it. And when I grew a moustache she made me – *asked me* to color it, too."

James studied Michael steadily. "I see. So which is it? Gun or knife?"

"What?"

"Which one does she use to keep you in line? Gun or knife?" James grinned. "Because you're not the sort of spineless bloke who'd let a woman control you barehanded."

Michael meant to keep his face blank, but he must have failed, because James shifted gears rapidly.

"That came out wrong. I just meant to say you're fit," James said. "Muscular enough to overpower any female. So it's hard for me to imagine wifey saying jump and you asking how high."

Michael said nothing.

"You know what? One of the things I love about

living in London," James announced, sounding like a radio advert, "is how you can get what you want, when you want. Feel like tweaking wifey's nose? Because if you do, I know just the ticket."

James had been right about tweaking Frannie's nose. She'd screamed – not cursed, not spluttered, but literally screamed when she saw Michael that next day. His conservative brown locks were missing, shaved down to a number 2 all over. Only a millimeter of ginger hair showed above his scalp. His moustache was gone.

"I look naked," Michael had told James as he stared at his face in the mirror.

"You look like a movie star." James was husky-voiced. It was no rent boy line; he was genuinely impressed. "Why the hell have you been hiding all this time?"

When Michael got home at 3 a.m., he'd found Frannie awake and pacing the kitchen. Leave it to her to skip Ambien the night he most needed her soundly asleep. Her recriminations were stern, bitter and perfectly reasonable.

"I'm fine. Worked late. Had a trip to the barber's. That's all," Michael said with false heartiness.

"*Michael.*" Frannie stared at him as if he'd changed his sex, sauntering in with penis gone and a sprightly new vagina between his thighs. "You can't be seen like this. What will people think?"

"I suppose they'll think I was after something different," Michael said over his shoulder. He headed upstairs to bed.

Germanotti was the next person to interrogate Michael. He found the new hair and missing moustache so inexplicable, so stunningly out of character, he verbally prodded at Michael all through lunch and dragged him to a gastro-pub for dinner.

"It's all to do with that bird from Brixton Park. Admit it." They sat waiting for fish and chips with a pint of bitter in front of Germanotti and a cola before Michael. "Seen her again, haven't you?"

"Four times now."

"And she got you to cut your hair?"

Michael nodded. It felt wrong, agreeing to Germanotti's assumptions without correcting him. Rent boy or no, James deserved basic human courtesy and respect. Besides, the lie wasn't only disrespectful to James. It was beneath Michael's dignity, too.

"All right." Germanotti took a long pull on his beer. "You know I have nothing. I'm a lifeless shell. A skeleton. Bleached bones circled by buzzards who won't even peck at me. Wendy snapped off my cock and keeps it in a pencil box. I visit it twice a year on

Christmas and my birthday. The only reason I don't top myself is in hopes you'll spill the sordid details and let me live vicariously through them."

Michael surprised himself by laughing aloud again – the second time in two days. "If your novel reads like that, I think it might sell."

"My novel is one long cry for help," Germanotti continued relentlessly, staring at Michael over the lip of his glass. "For Chrissake. Her name. Start with her name."

Michael drew in his breath. "His name is James."

Germanotti choked, recovering admirably as the waitress chose that moment to appear with their food. He even thanked her, offering up a friendly smile before locking eyes with Michael again.

"You sick twisted son of a bitch," he said levelly, shaking vinegar over his cod fillets and golden chips. "Tell me everything and don't leave out a single detail."

Michael didn't tell Germanotti everything, but he said enough to satisfy the other man's curiosity, at least for the moment. Michael was surprised to find he wasn't blushing. He blushed when a client or publisher praised a textbook manuscript, aware of its deficiencies, wondering if they had low standards or merely lied to be polite. He blushed when someone offered a small kindness, like opening a door when his hands were full. But he didn't blush at all as he skimmed his adventures with James – receiving oral sex at the Holiday Inn, giving it at the Nautilus, the massage-parlor treatment from Deepak and intercourse. Though Michael used a minimum of words, Germanotti obviously filled in the blanks. He was so attentive, his meal went cold.

"So, during all this debauchery, did you let James fuck you?"

Michael nodded.

"Was it good?"

Michael nodded again.

"Hang on." Rising, Germanotti went to the bar, waited briefly and brought back two shots of vodka. "I know, I know. But you'll hardly taste it. And goddamn it, *that* calls for a drink. You sick fuck. My God."

The shot of vodka went down as easily as promised. Michael felt slightly looser afterward, but not really impaired. He feared alcohol's tendency to amplify sadness, to stoke it into a crescendo, but nothing terrible happened. He just felt warm, happy, and grateful to his friend for listening. And the realization of that gratitude did, at last, make Michael begin to blush.

Germanotti did so little actual work at the company, Michael often forgot he was head of the science division and responsible for keeping all the biology textbooks current. So it was a pleasant surprise when Germanotti began talking quite rationally about Alfred Kinsey's sexuality research, including the Kinsey scale. By the end of the evening, they'd diverted to a complex disagreement about research samples and the efficacy of distributing questionnaires to volunteers. Michael went home in a fine mood and oddly comforted, though he couldn't say exactly why.

The next day at the office went normally until early afternoon. Realizing he needed to post a letter, Michael opened a drawer to look for stamps and found a bumper sticker atop his immaculate drawer organizer. It was a square rainbow flag.

Swiveling in his chair, he saw Germanotti at his own desk, hands laced behind his head, literally looking up at the ceiling and whistling. It was a cliché Michael had read about many times, but this was the first time in his life he'd ever seen anyone actually feign innocence that way.

Michael cleared his throat. Germanotti gave him a blank, practiced "Yes?" look. Then they were helpless with amusement, and Michael was surprised at the strength of his own throaty laugh.

For his next meet-up with James, Michael wanted nothing more than a repeat engagement at the Green Park Hilton. This time he'd masturbate a few hours before – on his lunch break, perhaps. Then when he penetrated James he'd be able to last, giving James plenty of time to warm up. Michael had read that sufficient prostate gland stimulation always led to ejaculation – this was physiology, not psychology. If he could find the right angle and the right amount of pressure, surely he could bring James to climax …

Excited by the prospect, Michael had tried to ring James. But James, usually quick to pick up or call back, didn't answer. After three tries, Michael texted him. A few hours later, he texted James again. Nothing. By the end of the day, Michael had no choice but to go home.

The next morning he tried again. Six calls between

nine o'clock in the morning and three in the afternoon. Nothing. And James had offered no e-mail, cheekily announcing he preferred to exist "off the grid ..."

Michael didn't know how he felt. Ignoring his current project, an exploration of religious texts for Year 10 pupils, Michael spent a good part of the day staring at the floor. He kept trying to determine how he felt, but no matter how he approached the question, the answer eluded him.

Around four o'clock he tried to ring James again. This time the other man answered on the second ring.

"Is everything all right?" Michael blurted. His heart hammered in his chest.

"Sure." James sounded odd, like he had a cold or a sore throat. "Fine. Why?"

"I – I was thinking we might meet up tonight. At the Hilton in Green Park."

There was a long pause. "Oh. Well. I'd like to, love, but something's come up. Trouble with a friend. I, um ... I'll be out of circulation for a while. Just temporary. Ring you up as soon as I'm back."

Michael felt like someone had stabbed him. "Oh." He tried to say more, but all that came out was, "Oh."

James sighed. "It's nothing tragic. Just – you know. Life. I've told you, I like you. I'll ring you up the second I'm back, I promise."

Michael gathered himself. He practiced the words in his head before he spoke them. "So are we finished, then?"

The silence seemed to go on forever. "Oh, fuck," James said at last. Was he crying? Was that why his voice sounded strange? "Fuck, fuck, fuck. You know that café. Not in Green Park. Outside the Nautilus?"

Michael did. They'd eaten there once, underwhelmed by the shabby décor and chilly, grease-caked sausages. "Yes."

"Meet you there in an hour."

Michael waited almost an hour and a half before James came through the door. He wore a zipped-up hoodie and dark glasses. Even from across the room, Michael could see the purple bruise on James's left cheek.

Michael stood up. "Who did this?" he whispered, throat tight, as James scooted into the booth's opposite side and tilted his head down.

"No idea," he said thickly, sounding even stranger than he had on the phone. "Never saw his face."

"Can I get you something, sweetheart?" the middle-aged waitress asked, pen poised above her notepad. She was plump and friendly, the sort of woman James liked to flirt with, but he barely gave her a glance.

"Two coffees," Michael said. He had a feeling they both might benefit from some caffeine. The second the waitress was out of earshot he said, "Tell me."

"The client didn't like me. So he knocked me about to show me how disappointing I was," James said in that same thick voice. He held his right hand over his mouth as he spoke. As if the words, once issued, would become all too real and so much more humiliating in the bargain.

"Take off the sunglasses," Michael said.

James obeyed. His nose was bruised but probably not broken. His left cheek was purple and swollen, some of the redness creeping up beneath his eye.

"It's not so bad." Michael was terrified by his own response, by the violent clenching inside his gut. "Tell me his name. Tell me who did it."

"I don't know!" James cried, hand over his mouth again. "I never sa—"

James broke off, shocked, as Michael pushed his hand away. James's four front teeth were gone. Behind his upper lip was a wide blood-red gap.

"Oh, no," Michael whispered. He meant the pain, not how it looked, but James's eyes filled with tears.

"I saw an emergency dentist," James said. "The doc sewed me up. Gave me antibiotic pills. But it'll be three weeks till I can get a cosmetic consultation. *Three weeks* till the initial visit, and God knows how much longer till this is fixed. And the pills ..." Breath hitching, James started to weep in earnest, tears rolling down his face. "They're making me sick. Making me shit all the time. It's disgusting! It's impossible! I can't work this way, Michael. No one would touch me. Oh, God, I'm so scared. I don't know what to do ..."

Michael found himself on the opposite side of the booth, arms sliding around James. Instinctively, he soothed the younger man as he might have soothed an animal, with a gentle rocking motion and low murmurs. Reappearing with their coffees, the waitress tried not to notice. Michael looked up at her, hoping she was a human being, that she could recognize the need of a fellow creature in distress, and wasn't disappointed.

"Does he need anything?" she whispered in Michael's ear.

"He'll be all right," Michael whispered back, ignoring the curiosity around him, some of it contemptuous, some of it prurient. "Thank you."

"I didn't deserve this," James wept against him as the waitress checked on her other tables. "I was trying to be what he wanted …"

"I know." Michael held James tighter. "I know."

"You have to let go. People will see."

"I don't care."

James sniffed again, tried to rally and fell into fresh sobs. "Oh, Michael, I'm sorry. I don't know what to do."

Michael ran a hand over James's thick brown hair. "It's all right. I do."

Paul Beckman, D.D.S., A.A.C.D., was more than a bespoke cosmetic dentist with a posh London office. He was Michael's brother-in-law.

It was complicated. Frannie's sister Caitlin married Paul Beckman fifteen years ago, when he was fresh out of training. For all that time, she'd been not only his wife but his chief dental hygienist. Then a few months ago, they'd announced their pending divorce on

Facebook. No recriminations were evident on either side; until recently, Caitlin had continued working at the office. Frannie, never close to her sister, didn't have the full story, only that Paul was sleeping with one of his younger hygienists. Michael had no idea what had happened, nor did he care. Paul's work was top-drawer, and he was the only dentist Michael knew that would meet them after hours and see James privately.

Not wanting to hover, Michael spent the initial consultation in Paul's office. He was on the computer researching his current project – textbook creation could be oddly soothing – when Paul entered.

"All right. The doctor who removed James's broken teeth and sewed up his gums made a botch of it, but nothing I can't fix. There are two ways to go. The most affordable option is a bridge." Paul used an oversized plastic model to illustrate. "Essentially, a partial denture plate. It goes in and out and has to be cleaned, but should look good. The downside is the upkeep and some loss of functionality. No more corn on the cob or toffee apples.

"The other option, the Mercedes, would be implants. I'd take impressions, order four prosthetics and implant them. After a few weeks he wouldn't know the difference from his own teeth. Except these will be porcelain-veneered and never decay or turn yellow. So better than nature." Paul took a breath. "I asked which he preferred, and he said it was all up to you."

"Implants."

"Right." Paul named a sum. "That's for everything. The molds, the prosthetics, the oral surgery and the follow-up. Also the meds."

Michael passed a hand over his hair's soft spikiness. For the second time that week, he was grateful Frannie never snooped in his finances. "I'll need to transfer some funds. But I'll have it for you by tomorrow morning."

Paul nodded. He half-rose, then sat down again, looking Michael in the eye. "I realize we don't know one another very well …"

That was true. Michael generally saw Paul four times a year – Christmas, Frannie's birthday, and his semi-annual teeth cleanings.

"But really," Paul continued, "what the hell's going on? I barely recognized you. And James. Who is he?"

"Son of a friend." Michael spoke the lie he'd concocted. "He's been in trouble. Going through a rough patch. I said I'd help him get on his feet."

Paul stared at him. Michael stared back. Heaping on additional details would only make him sound more like the liar he was.

"Son of a friend," Paul said at last, still holding Michael's gaze. "That's interesting. Because after spending ten minutes with James – talking to him – I took him for your rent boy."

Michael still didn't answer. Should he come clean or continue to stonewall? Would Paul refuse to do the procedure if Michael admitted the truth?

"*Is* he your rent boy?" Paul asked.

"Yes."

"You're not the one who knocked his teeth out, are you?"

Michael was shocked by the question. "Of course not." Even at the gym he never put on boxing gloves and pounded the heavy bag. He'd never struck another person in his life. "Why would you think that?"

Paul shrugged. "There's such a thing as suppressed rage. There's such a thing as sublimated murderous impulses. And then there's you, Michael. I can imagine you punching somebody's lights out. Pretty easily, in fact." Paul waved a hand. "It doesn't matter. That kid needs his mouth worked on and I'll do it. I'll even give you the usual fifteen percent family discount. But Jesus, Michael. Weren't you afraid I'd figure it out? That I'd tell Frannie?"

This time Michael shrugged. "Crossed my mind. But you're the best. Thought I'd risk it."

Paul didn't answer right away. Then he stood up. "Fine. I'm flattered. And what you do is your business. What James does for a living is his business. But this is oral surgery. Unless he can show me a blood test done in the last thirty days that defines his STD status, including HIV, I won't perform the procedure."

Michael gave James the news about the blood test himself. James, unable to produce such evidence, was unsurprised. "I can't abide those clinics. All those nosy questions. Nurses staring at me like I'm a zoo animal. I've been inside once or twice and always left without getting stuck."

"It isn't an unreasonable request. You need to do it."

"No, I can just wait for my NHS dentist appointment. It won't be so long. And if I go through the system, it won't cost you anything." James's eyes were painfully wide, transmitting the fear he fought to keep out of his voice. "How much does Dr. Beckman mean to charge for my implants?"

"Enough," Michael smiled. "Let me worry about that. As for the test – I'll go with you. We'll get tested together."

It took a bit more convincing, but the next morning James turned up outside the clinic, still in his hoodie and sunglasses. Michael, who'd arrived in his usual work attire, felt as overdressed as he'd been the night he met James in Brixton Park.

James started out nervous and progressed to near spastic when the secretary passed him a three-page questionnaire. He stared at it for a moment, then placed it defiantly on the floor. "I'm not doing that. I can barely see it. Don't have my contacts in."

Michael, who excelled at filling in forms and was already finished with his, put out his hand. "Give it over."

Asking the questions and jotting down the answers taught Michael a lot about James. He'd recently turned twenty-two, but never mentioned his birthday. He'd been born in Scotland but his parents had moved first to Manchester, then London, before James was five years old. They divorced when James was seven. His father was a mason; his mother was a hairdresser. He'd stopped going to school around age thirteen and the truant officer, his cousin, had covered for him. For a long time he'd apprenticed with his mum, sweeping up hair clippings and giving old women shampoos. But the work hadn't suited him, so James teamed up with his father and did masonry for a year. Then sometime around age sixteen, he discovered he could make as much or more seducing men in clubs, bars, even street corners.

"So you knew you were homosexual at sixteen?" Michael asked.

James shrugged. "Not really. I knew men liked me. Hadn't quite decided what I liked yet." His discomfort had lessened considerably since Michael took custody of his paperwork. "Did you know you were heterosexual at sixteen?"

Michael smiled. "I knew I liked girls. And once in awhile – this was a deep dark secret, I never told another living soul – I was curious about boys. But after I met Frannie and started getting sex regularly, I never thought about boys again. Not until you."

"Labels are tedious," James sighed. "I mean, I know I'm a pouf because of what's in here." He tapped his chest. "When I was eighteen I fell in love with a bloke named Kevin. Until then I'd fucked – I don't know, four or five girls, and had a good time. But when I fell for Kevin, I knew I was a pouf. And it felt so right I didn't give a damn."

"What happened with him?"

"Kev? Oh. Nothing much." James glanced shyly at Michael, as if already regretting what he'd said. "Once we got drunk and made out. Other than that, Kev's always been with someone else. Usually a big bloke with muscles on his muscles and a cock like – well, yours." James grinned, hand snaking up to cover his mouth.

"None of that." Michael pushed the other man's hand away from his face. "Bad habit."

"I look like a freak."

"You're still beautiful. Just injured." Michael drew in his breath. "I always thought of myself as heterosexual. Until I met you. You arouse me like no one else."

"How many people have you fucked?"

"Two," Michael lied. "Frannie and you."

"Well, then, I'd say the jury's out. The good news – it doesn't matter. If you adore being married to wifey, so be it. If you like fucking me on the side, so be it. It's all about personal truth, mate."

Michael thought about that phrase, "personal truth." It was a long time until the frowning, harried nurse call him back – almost an hour – but even by then, he had no idea what a "personal truth" was, much less if he had one.

The test results came back around noon. The Nautilus's bar – called the Seashore – opened at 1 p.m. Michael maneuvered James inside and ordered him a margarita. "Make it with Patron Silver," he told the bartender.

"You don't even drink. How do you know about Patron Silver?" James sounded bleak.

"I hear things." Specifically, Michael heard things

from Germanotti, who knew all his wife's favorite cocktails. But to reveal the source of enlightenment would spoil the mystery.

James said nothing until Michael returned from the bar with a cola for himself and that Patron Silver margarita for James. James finished the drink, head bobbing to the dance beat, trying not to make eye contact with Michael. He fetched another from the bar and drank it. Half way through his third, he announced, "I am a whore. A dirty, diseased whore."

"Hush." Michael leaned over the table, trying to intimidate with his eyebrows and his shoulders, wondering if it were time to cut James off.

"No, really. I have the paperwork to prove it," James slurred, sipping the margarita through its pink straw. "I have HSV-2. Isn't that romantic? Sexy?"

"You're not the only person to have genital herpes. The incidence is at least one in six males in Britain. I checked."

"You'll have it next," James predicted, pulling the straw out of his drink and poking it at Michael. "The gift that goes on giving. I don't understand how I could have it and never know. I mean once – *once* – I got itchy for a day or so. Before I could get an appointment, I went back to normal. Figured I dodged a bullet and never thought about it again." James sank half the margarita in one gulp. "Seriously, Michael, if you stick around, you'll catch it from me. I'm a dirty, diseased whore. Bet you never thought about the consequences when you chatted me up in that park."

"I did," Michael said gently.

James stared at him.

"I knew what you did for a living. I knew I was about to have sex with a stranger. I would have had to be deaf, dumb and dead not to understand what I was risking. Thirty years of public service announcements," Michael said. "Not all of them fell on deaf ears."

James, who'd already cried once, looked ready to tear up again. Michael reached across the table and touched the other man's hand. "If I contract herpes, I'll deal with it. My point is, I knew the risks and I chose to go forward. Wouldn't even let you wear a condom while I filleted you."

James made a startled noise. Then, despite his red eyes and boozy melancholy, he flashed that grin. It wasn't gorgeous now. It was a parody. Yet inexplicably, Michael found he still liked it.

"First time you've ever joked around with me."

"First time I've ever joked around at all. Now," Michael said briskly. "Let's get you some food on your stomach before you start vomiting."

But the hamburger and chips came too late. James ate half of it at a fair clip, then disappeared into the men's room for ten minutes. "It's not just the margaritas," he gasped when he returned to the table, translucently pale and shaking. "It's those damn antibiotics."

"Right. Come on, follow me. You've had a grim couple of days and I'm putting you to bed."

James, still tipsy despite all the purging, let Michael lead him to the tube station. They disembarked at Shepherd's Bush and walked to an old building called the Highland Arms. The stairs gave James the dry heaves, but eventually they made it to the third floor.

Once inside No. 32, Michael half-carried James through the small sitting room and into the bedroom.

The bed, just an IKEA frame, a mattress, and white cotton sheets, seemed to be exactly what James needed. He stretched out on his back and groaned with what sounded like pleasure.

"Oh, this is so much better than my fucking futon. I'll be crippled before I'm thirty sleeping on that thing. And I haven't really slept since that bastard broke my teeth ... I keep dreaming he'll come back and kill me ..."

"He's not coming back," Michael said in the same matter-of-fact tone he'd used when six-year-old Edward was plagued by nightmares. "You're safe here and you need to sleep." Michael started to undo James's belt, thinking the other man would sleep more comfortably in just his T-shirt and shorts, but James flinched.

"Sorry." Michael withdrew his hands. "Look, I have to at least check in at the office, so I'll be gone for a while. Stay put till I get back and I'll order us some dinner."

"Michael." James's eyes were red again, tears spilling over. "I owe you. I know I do. But I don't ... I just don't think I can ..."

"I said dinner. That's all."

"But – what is this place? Where are we?"

"My new flat. Now go to sleep."

Michael worked on his current textbook – the overview of world religions – until his boss, Peter, returned from his usual late lunch. Not long ago Peter had allowed one of the more junior writers to work from home most days, turning up at the office only to make presentations and attend meetings. That writer, though competent, frequently missed deadlines and sometimes needed coaching from the senior staff to finish his projects. The only reason he'd been permitted to work from home was, surely, his friendship with Peter. Michael knew he was a far better choice – not only was he capable of supervising himself, but he was the company's most prolific author. After bestowing such a plum on a comparatively undeserving employee, Peter would have no choice but to say yes.

"Absolutely not. And frankly, I'm surprised at you," Peter told Michael, smiling in his usual secretive way. "Perhaps it's time you came clean to me. Is something wrong at home?"

Michael waited, unsure why Peter would ask that. Germanotti was many things, but he was no grass. He hadn't gossiped about James – Michael would have staked his life on it.

"You've radically changed your appearance. You pushed for the world religions survey when you knew I wanted you to handle the machine shop primer. And today you buggered off without so much as an apology."

"I told you. It was medical."

"You don't look sick to me." Peter gave him that secretive smile again. Not a writer, not a teacher, and not an educational theorist, he'd been hired by the company for his expertise as an MBA. It pleased him to look down his nose at subordinates who didn't understand the value of money, who hadn't attended management seminars and motivational talks. "So what's really happening? Why do you need more time at home?"

Michael, who only wanted to spend his workdays in his new flat with James, fought back a smile at the notion of voluntarily spending additional time with Frannie. And she would like it no better, he realized. Possibly less.

"If employees are receiving permission to work from home, there's no one on staff more deserving than me," Michael said truthfully. "I've never missed a deadline. I've assisted the art department and the layout team voluntarily to make sure an excellent product goes out. I've written more textbooks than anyone here. And I'm your most senior writer, besides Germanotti." Who, Michael added mentally, would suck on the barrel of a handgun before he'd waste his precious workdays at home.

Peter sighed. "I was hoping you'd open up to me. Let me help you. But if you prefer to be unemotional and blunt, fine. I'll give it to you straight." He leaned across the desk at Michael. "You've never struck me as someone devoted to protecting the organization. And in the current economic climate, there's no more important value than protecting this organization. You're not editorial or management material. Even among the writers, you're not a team player. So no, I see no reason to reward your disconnection by permitting further isolation. The global economy is tanking, Michael." Peter gave a sad shake of the head. "Pick up a newspaper sometime. Writers are standing in bread lines. You can be replaced."

Michael digested Peter's words carefully. His rational mind tried to make sense of it all, to decide if the other man's assessment was accurate or fair. Below that, something else was brewing inside him. He didn't quite know what. But there had to be a name for it, this fire and certainty and elation and ferocity ...

It hit Michael all at once. Peter didn't necessarily believe everything he'd said. He was fucking with Michael. Fucking with him the way a cat shifted a mouse from paw to paw, first a plaything, then a meal. Not because he would receive any measurable benefit from refusing to let Michael work from home. Just because he enjoyed the sensation.

"I see." Michael stood up.

"I meant what I said," Peter called after him, trying to sound friendly and fatherly again, though he was at least five years Michael's junior. "Talk to me anytime! Come clean!"

Michael went back to his desk. He unpinned the calendar, a Christmas gift from Frannie, and dropped it in the rubbish bin. The mouse pad, one of Vivian's school projects from years ago, went there, too. Going through his desk drawers, he retrieved his spare change, the postage stamps he'd purchased with his own money, his Excellence in Technical Writing plaques (all four of them) and two Cadbury Fruit and Nut bars he'd been saving since Easter ...

"Michael?" Germanotti closed his Internet poker

game. "What the hell are you doing?"

"Michael?" Peter called from his office door. "What's this, then?"

"Per our discussion," Michael said, not looking over his shoulder as he marched toward the exit. "Replace me."

The idea of taking the tube home was unbearable, so Michael called Frannie and made up a story about working late and staying nearby as part of an intensive research session. He'd done it twice before to help Germanotti finish overdue projects, so it wasn't unprecedented. Frannie's displeasure surprised him.

"You know, I don't exist just to keep your house and rear your children," she snapped. "I'm not on your staff like Caitlin worked for Paul."

Michael went cold at the mention of Paul. For a moment he thought his brother-in-law had actually told Frannie about James.

"You want us to spend more time together?"

She sighed. "I don't want to end up like Caitlin. She's starting over at thirty-seven. Probably never find another husband while Paul can go on fucking young girls till he's dead with old age." Silence. Then: "Is that why you cut your hair and shaved your moustache? To be more attractive to young women?"

The backhanded compliment surprised him. He

couldn't remember the last time Frannie had so much as implied he was attractive. "No. That's not why I did it, I promise."

"You know I hate ginger hair."

"I know. Germanotti's waving me over. Have to go." He disconnected. Michael had never been one to toss around "I love you" as an end to trivial conversations and Frannie, equally reserved, never expected it. Even during their courtship he'd never said those words, though he'd been wildly infatuated. One night she'd announced, "You love me, I know you do." Finding no reason to disagree, he'd presented her with an engagement ring the next day. And when Edward was born, he'd held the bundle in his arms and whispered, "I love you." He'd done the same with Viv. Those had been the best moments of his marriage, creating two new individuals with Frannie. Maybe he did need to spend more time with his family. His kids, at least.

When James woke up, they shared a nice takeaway dinner – Indian green curry, tandoori scallops and shatkora along with some white rice and mango chutney. They drank iced water. This time James managed to keep everything down, though the antibiotics still troubled his stomach. Michael had furnished the place only sparingly – one IKEA sofa, two torchière lamps, a flat screen TV hung opposite the sofa and a Blu-ray player. James, already aware of Michael's detached house in Brixton, found the new flat impossibly posh.

"So you're a rich bloke," he said as Michael stowed the leftovers in the fridge.

"I'm a comfortable bloke."

"What do you do for a living? Wait, don't tell me. I'll guess." James squinted at Michael as if X-raying him. "You're a university professor."

"A writer."

"Really? Like *Harry Potter* and *Twilight*?"

"Like textbooks. *Introduction to Biology. Fundamentals of Ecology, Second Edition.* And so on."

James visibly deflated. "Never figured you for the sadist type."

Michael chuckled. "I guess for those who didn't enjoy school, that's exactly what I am."

"And people pay lots of money for textbooks?" James tried not to sound skeptical.

"Not really. My money comes from my mum. She died when I was five."

"How?"

"Wrongful death." Michael brought his glass of iced water over to the sofa and sat down beside James. "She had lung cancer. Never smoked a day, it just happened. The hospital was meant to remove her diseased left lung. They removed her right by mistake." Michael couldn't pretend an excess of emotion where none existed. He didn't remember his mother, not really. He still felt the lack of her, the void, but it was amorphous. Probably boys who'd never known their mums felt more or less the same. "Anyway, she lived long enough with one cancerous lung to sue and receive a settlement. The money came to me as a trust fund. It's always been there, a crutch, something I could turn to if everything else went wrong."

"How often have you dipped into it?"

"Three times. To make a down payment on the

house in Brixton. To rent this flat. And ..." Michael smiled, unsure how to say the rest properly.

"Oh. Yes. To fix up your toothless, diseased whore."

"Please don't start that again." Michael was still unsettled by what happened at his former workplace and eager to forget it. But dealing with it would have been so much easier if he knew what he felt – anger, sadness, rage, contrition or fear. Surely if he could name what he felt, he could process it. In textbooks, defining a basic vocabulary was often the first step.

"Let's watch a movie." Michael switched on the streaming service. "You pick."

James's entertainment tastes were quite different from Frannie's. She tended to enjoy human dramas where people lied, slept around or even murdered for dense psychosocial reasons. Or else she liked highbrow romances where repressed men in puffy shirts made love to dowerless girls and/or governesses. James preferred cars, guns, slow-motion stunts and explosions. He chose something Michael had heard of but Frannie had never let him watch, a violent fable starring Angelina Jolie, and they spent the next ninety minutes immersed in gunplay, assassination and cataclysmic stunts.

"I love this part." James, who'd apparently memorized the movie, insisted Michael watch a particular sequence carefully. "I could do that. Shoot the wings off a fly. If this fucking pussy country let people buy guns and ammo at Marks & Spencer the way they can in America ..."

Michael fought back a laugh. Had he ever in his life enjoyed so much free-floating enthusiasm? Even injured and depressed, James put him to shame. "I'm not sure anyone could shoot the wings off a fly. You might find it especially difficult. You'd certainly need your corrective lenses."

"Hey?" James shot Michael an uncomprehending look. "My vision's perfect, mate. 20/20. That fly's wings are toast." He pantomimed shooting an imaginary insect with his hands, then happily resumed immersion in the movie.

Afterward, James was sleepy and Michael was, too. He had no intention of pressuring James for sex. Stripping only to his undershirt and shorts, he doused the lights and got into bed. Not long after, James crept out of the small bathroom still fully dressed and stretched out on the sofa.

Michael fell asleep assuming James would come to bed when he was ready. But when he awakened at half-five, he found James curled up on the sofa asleep. There was something almost feline about James in sleep, chin tucked, knees drawn up against to his chest. Looking down at him, Michael felt a spasm of desire below the waist. He felt something else, too, harder to define. A gentleness quite apart from his physical response. Taken together those two responses – one feather-soft and considerate, the other visceral, hungry, full of personal need – confused Michael even more than his tumult of emotion after walking off the job.

He touched James's cheek, hoping the other man would wake and fancy some type of intimacy. Intercourse was his first choice, but fellatio or mutual masturbation would be almost as welcome ...

"No," James whispered, jerking awake. "No!"

"Sorry," Michael breathed, pulling away. "I'm sorry." Seeing James's wide eyes, his obvious fear, Michael didn't wait for an explanation. He headed into the shower. When he emerged, James was pouring coffee.

"It started when I was twelve," he said, pushing a mug toward Michael. "My uncle Kirk. He came into my bedroom and started touching me while I slept. I woke up and he said if I told anyone, he'd say he caught me doing something dirty. Then he ran his hands over me from stem to stern. I still dream about it, hands groping me while I sleep. In the dream there's no safe place. Not even my own bed in my own room. Nowhere to let down my guard."

Michael busied himself with the coffee, grateful for a task. He found the sugar, added it, then found the half-and-half, pouring it in as well. "How far did it go?"

"He fucked me." James took a sip of coffee. "Lots of times. Then one day I went mental on the bastard – still can't remember what I said – and after I hit him and threatened him, he finally beat it. But by then, other men were starting to come on to me. Offering me money for sex. Finally, I realized … well. Personal truth. That's just who I was. What I was good for."

"A whore for randy older men?"

"Yeah. Like you." As soon as he uttered the words, James looked genuinely shocked at himself. "I – I'm sorry. I'm a bit … unhinged. Never thought a client would do this to me," he said, gesturing toward his mouth. "Angry, I guess. Though I have no idea why I'd take it out on you."

"Because I'm a client, too. But James. This – what's

happening now – isn't about what we usually do. I'm not buying you. You don't have to keep a running tally."

"If it's not about sex ... then what?"

Michael modulated his breathing. This would be taking a chance. But he could withstand the truth, he knew he could. He could ask James to be honest and not fear it would break him.

"It's about friendship. I think of you as a friend. What we did before – I'd like to go back to it, whenever you're ready. But until then, I want you to stay here, James. Get better. Spend time with me. Unless ... unless it's too much. Unless you don't think of me the same way."

"I thought of you as a client," James said softly. "Till you rang me up. Till I said I was out of commission and you asked if we were finished. I felt – I don't know. I thought maybe it would hurt you, wondering why I disappeared. So I met you in the restaurant. Not because I expected you to help me. I just didn't want to leave you in pain." James took a deep breath. "I don't deserve you as a friend."

"I don't deserve you, either," Michael said. It was the most he could manage. There was more inside him, he knew there was, but it was like staring at the white digital page when he tried to write a piece of fiction. A disconnect that made communication impossible. So he kept his silence, finished his coffee and decided to purchase a laptop. He'd need a computer to update his resume and search for a new job.

James's first official appointment with Dr. Beckman was scheduled for ten o'clock. He'd been given an information packet with forms to fill in and what looked like written directions to the office from multiple points in the city. James planned to do what he always did – get on the tube, charm people into guiding him, and turn up for his appointment with the forms conveniently forgotten. But Michael opened up the packet and spread the papers across the minimalist IKEA coffee table. "Let's get these done."

Michael filled in most of them from memory, getting a few details from James. Then he bundled them together along with James's test results from the clinic. "Now. How are you at studying schematics? Like fire escape routes in buildings?"

"Fine," James mumbled. He was as embarrassed now as he'd been over his missing teeth. Most people assumed he was stupid, including people he considered pals like Deepak and Kevin. But not one of them had ever deduced just how stupid he really was.

"Take the tube back to Belgravia. There's a McDonald's just outside. Cross the street to the McDonald's and follow this route," Michael sketched a path with several turns, "until you end up at Paul's office. There's a uniformed doorman and some truly hideous potted plants outside."

"Thanks." James took the map, suddenly aware he'd

be going back to the office in the same clothes. Would they notice? Would they laugh at him? Pity him?

His throat constricted. Next thing he knew he was crying again, and when Michael put an arm around him, he didn't shrug him off.

"It's why you left school, isn't it?" Michael said.

"It was fucking torture," James choked, sobbing even harder. "A daily exploration of how fucking retarded I am! I just gave up. You must … someone like you must …" More sobs. "I can't believe you write fucking textbooks."

"Well, I sort of gave myself the sack yesterday," Michael said. "So just at the moment, I have no occupation at all." He explained the situation as James pulled himself together. James wasn't stiff about crying when he needed to. Sometimes a good cry was the best remedy, as his mum said, and he tended to agree. But he didn't want to spend every moment pissing and moaning to Michael. The man had problems of his own. And he was the sort of person who liked to help, who liked to feel useful …

"Could you teach me to read?"

"I'm not sure." Michael's tone suggested he was already weighing the question. "Were you diagnosed with dyslexia?"

"Severe," James said. "Rhymes with stupid, just means I get more from being hit over the head with a book than looking at what's inside it. Oh, and they said I have ADD, too." He lit a cigarette, his first of the day, and took a long, grateful drag. "But listen, mate, I once sucked a geezer for twenty minutes to get him off. The clock was just over his shoulder and I timed it.

Attention deficit?" He blew out a plume of smoke. "I don't think so."

The appointment was easier than James imagined. The staff was pleasant, he flirted with everyone, including Dr. Beckman, and submitted to the molds, a cleaning and a lecture about flossing with good grace. It would take a week for the implants to arrive. Until then, James would confine himself to closed-mouth smiles and ducking his head. It was a strange feeling, being ashamed of his looks. Until his injury, they were the only attribute he was truly proud of.

He swung by his flat and found an eviction notice on the door. That was no surprise. Inside he loaded up two tote bags with his relevant possessions – three more pairs of jeans, two shirts, socks, underwear, condoms, lube, an MP3 player, ear buds, comb, shampoo, conditioner and a box of frosted cherry Pop-Tarts. He left his old toothbrush behind; Dr. Beckman's office had given him a kit with a fancy toothbrush and a tube of organic peppermint toothpaste. The rest, including his futon and his old TV, he never cared to see again.

When James returned to the flat in Shepherd's Bush, he found Michael sitting on the floor assembling a new piece of IKEA furniture. The flat consisted of a sitting room connected to a small kitchen, with a bedroom and toilet to the right. The only other room, hardly bigger than a loo, was doubtless meant to serve as an office or storage space. The twin-sized bed frame Michael was putting together would fit inside, but only just. There would be no room for anything else.

"Planning on asking your kids round?"

"Here? No. This will be yours, when you want it."

James didn't know what to say. No more crying, no more pissing and moaning, he told himself sternly. Noticing the MacBook on the coffee table, he went to it, studying the symbols on the digital desktop. Probably he'd never learn to actually read an entire book from start to finish. But if he could just pick up enough to have a proper e-mail address like the whole rest of the world, to search for cinema times and takeaway menus and porn ...

He clicked around, opening and closing programs, wishing he could actually use the damn thing. "So you can search for a job online?"

"I could. But turns out I won't be. I told you about Peter. Well, his boss, Philip, called me while you were out. And apparently ..." Michael shot James a sidelong smile. "I am now working from home. I'll have to go in occasionally for meetings and such. Otherwise, I'll compose my textbooks from here."

"You badass motherfucker," James grinned. "You know what you did? You cut off Peter's bollocks and fed them to him."

Michael only smiled. He was more than an attractive man, James realized suddenly. He was growing more handsome by the day as his ginger hair came in. He'd grown a little beard stubble, too. The moustache had made him look old and constipated. The all-over stubble made him look edible.

James was eating a frosted cherry Pop-Tart when he realized what Michael was installing on the inside of the small bedroom's door. It was a stainless steel deadbolt.

"Hey. What happened this morning – don't over

think it," James said, alarmed. "I was just startled. I'm not afraid of you, Michael. That lock is way over the top."

Michael kept right on drilling the second hole. "The lock isn't practical. It's symbolic. If you want to shoot the bolt, you can. Simple as that."

As a boy James would have given anything for a place of his own to sleep, a way to keep people out. For a moment he was stunned that Michael understood. Then it came clear to James, as basic words occasionally did if he stared at them long enough and really tried.

"What my uncle did to me. Something like that happened to you."

Eyes still on his work, Michael nodded.

James didn't try to touch Michael, didn't try to make him discuss it. Michael had loosened up considerably, but he was still stiff and robotic at times, the way he'd been when he stripped for Deepak's massage. With Michael, confessions would never come easily, if at all.

"If you ever want to tell me, you can." James let the invitation hang between them for a moment. Then he thrust the Pop-Tart box under Michael's nose. "Fancy one? Healthy stuff. Nine essential vitamins and minerals."

James saw Michael's eyes shine as he removed a foil-wrapped packet, but James pretended not to notice. The afternoon passed companionably without further mention. Around five o'clock, Michael took the tube back to Brixton. James sat up watching action movies and eating the rest of the Indian takeaway. He tried to have a wank, but not even fantasies about Kevin stoked his engine. He was too aware of his missing teeth, afraid of what Kev would think to see him this way. Finally James sorted through the streaming service until he located some porn. It was boy-girl, not his usual cup of tea, though the woman's tits were natural and quite nice. And the man, Mr. Horse Cock, was slim yet well muscled, with short hair and a slight beard ...

One of these days I'll fuck Michael blind. Give it to him like no one has. Make him glad to know me, James thought, surprised by his own randiness, and came in record time. Then he stretched out in his tiny new bedroom, closed the door, shot the bolt and fell into perfect dreamless sleep.

James awakened around seven, not long before Michael turned up. They had breakfast in a café, then went grocery shopping.

"It's weird, the things I can make sense of," James confided. "I know that sign says milk. I know that box says Frosted Flakes. I've seen them on telly so much, the pictures and the words, I get it. But give me a long sentence or a whole page and I lose the plot straight away."

"I read up on dyslexia last night," Michael said, frowning at the meat section. "Can you cook?"

"Sure. Mum taught me."

"Then pick out whatever food you'll feel like cooking. Anyway, I'm not qualified to teach you. There are specific strategies for dyslexics. We need to hook you up with an adult literacy program. A certified tutor should help a lot."

"I'd rather you do it," James sighed, weighing one package of minced beef against another.

Michael shook his head. "James. You're not stupid. But you have a disorder and you'll get frustrated trying to overcome it. I'd rather you get frustrated with a stranger, take out your anger on him, then come home to me."

As Michael worked on his survey of world religions textbook, James whipped up bangers and mash for lunch. When they sat down to eat, James was pleased to watch Michael savor every bite, then swoop in for seconds. Fit as he was, the man verged on too thin.

While Michael resumed his work, James took the tube to the section of Wapping Michael had identified, following the drawing Michael provided. James found the Adult Learning Annex with no difficulty. Part of him suspected he'd be turned away within a week for stupidity. Part of him fantasized about becoming their most distinguished pupil, absorbing his remedial lessons in record time. Each idea was frightening in its own way. But in the end, James forced himself to enter, started by apologizing for his missing teeth, and let an intern assess his needs. He gave his details and was swiftly accepted. The program directors sent him home with several slim books, each individual page featuring several related photos and one or two words.

"Figured they'd start me with Winnie-the-Pooh," James admitted to Michael. "But look." He opened a book to a photo of a large bottle of milk. Beneath it the word MILK was printed in capital letters.

"Already know this one," James said, tapping a finger against his temple. "Ahead of the curve."

"I'm proud of you."

"Because I know the word milk?" James scoffed, wondering if Michael meant to take the mickey.

"No. Because you went and signed up. When I was a boy, I never learned to swim. But when my kids were little, they kept begging me to take them to the pool. I finally had to sign up for an adult swim class." Michael smiled. "It was one of the hardest things I ever did. Giving up my dignity, flailing around and letting an instructor teach me something most kids do instinctively. The instructor told me adults usually give up after one lesson."

"They told me the same thing at the Learning Annex," James said. "Most people bugger off as soon as the lessons shift from single words to sentences. So can you swim now?"

"Yes."

"Brilliantly?"

"No. But good enough not to embarrass my kids. And that was the point."

James cooked dinner – squash casserole, his mum's recipe – and then they settled back on the sofa for a movie. Afterward, James slid into Michael's arms. He wasn't sure how far he wanted things to go. But he wanted to be held, and he wasn't disappointed. They watched another movie like that, Michael on his back, James on top on him, cheek pressed against the other man's chest. He liked the feel on Michael's fingers against his scalp, down his neck, along the length of his spine. He hardly paid any attention to the movie, enthralled by being held without any sexual overtures, without dirty talk or traveling hands. Michael was semi-hard, had been that way for a while, yet he said nothing.

"Want to watch some porn?" James whispered as the movie's credits began to roll.

Michael nodded. Shyly, he kissed James's forehead. James responded by pressing their mouths together, kissing the other man until they were both breathless. Then he took the remote and started searching. As he'd noted the previous night, the streaming service's basic porn feed was geared toward the mainstream. Currently two blonde women, one lithe and delectable, the other curvaceous with huge enhanced tits, were having a food fight in a kitchen. Covered with batter, flour and sugar crystals, they started to make out, then to clean each other with their mouths. The lithe girl spread her legs as the curvaceous one licked thick yellow batter away, revealing the pink beneath.

"Fancy a little girl on girl, do you?" James whispered, caressing Michael's hard-on.

"It's nice," Michael murmured, gaze shifting to James. "I'm beginning to wonder if there's anything I don't fancy."

"We could find a girl and share her," James said. "You take her pussy. I'll take her ass. Fuck her so hard our cocks meet in the middle."

Michael made a little sound. James grinned.

"You are so easy. I swear I could make you come just by talking," he whispered in Michael's ear. "But I'd rather …"

"What?"

James finished the sentence that had come spontaneously to his lips. "I'd rather have you the old-fashioned way."

Michael undid his belt, sliding out of his trousers. He was slipping off his boxer shorts when James realized his condoms were in his little bedroom. "I need ..."

"Please," Michael said, lifting his face for a kiss. James couldn't deny him, couldn't deny his own urgency, but he had to repeat the truth.

"I don't have a condom or lube ..."

Michael already had James's jeans around his ankles, had his shorts down and cock out. He guided that hard member down to his asshole and pressed against it, opening himself, letting a millimeter of James slip inside.

James moaned. They both knew he had HSV-2. Part of James considered unprotected sex ludicrous, indefensible. The other part thought this was Michael's way of expressing something he couldn't put in words. The pleasure enveloping the head of James's cock, slightly inside Michael, was radically different without that familiar latex shield. Michael was hot, tight and rough, exciting James all the way back to his own asshole. When he pushed in harder, Michael cried out, teeth clenched.

"Does it hurt too much?"

"I like it," Michael gasped. "Harder."

James took a deep breath. Then he pushed into Michael as hard as he could, burying himself up to his balls. Michael made a choked sound, pain mingled with pleasure, even as his cock jerked and emitted a molten white pearl.

"You want my cock, don't you?"

Michael nodded, eyes shut, torso lifting as he wrapped his legs around James.

"Say it."

"I want your cock."

"Say it!"

"I want your cock so bad – oh – oh God—"

Michael broke off as James hit his rhythm, thrusting according to Michael's gasps.

"You want my cock more than those sweet little pussies?"

"Yes."

"Why?"

"Fuck me," Michael moaned, lower half lifting even more, gripping James's upper arms with both hands.

"What?"

"*Fuck me*," Michael cried, almost sobbing with desire.

James was committed then, pounding in and out like a jackhammer, pressure rising in his lower belly. He's so close, James thought, biting his lower lip with pride.

"James," Michael said distinctly. When James heard his own name, something happened. His inner landscape tilted and his hidden mechanisms halted, tripped by some mysterious kill-switch. As James came, cock pumping, belly hard as a rock with shocked pleasure, he felt Michael clamp down inside, his own member squirting hard.

"Oh God," James sighed, collapsing into Michael's arms. It was a long time before Michael could speak.

"That was real," he said at last.

"Yes."

"We came at the same time."

"I didn't think it was possible," James admitted. He kissed Michael then, long and wet, his missing teeth occurring to him only as an afterthought. "You really don't mind?"

Michael was confused.

"How I look," James said, pointing toward his mouth.

"Of course not. I love you," Michael said, fingers in James's hair and kissing him hard. But after that they soon parted, Michael getting dressed again to ride the tube to Brixton, James taking refuge in his small bedroom, each pretending the words had never been said at all.

The rest of the week was nice. Michael enjoyed leaving Frannie each morning, supposedly to go to his office, only to turn up at his flat and work from there. James was invested in his literacy program, spending three hours a day in class and the rest of the time trying to make sense of his homework. Michael didn't interfere or offer advice. He didn't know much about dyslexia, but he knew the sort of reading encouragement he'd once offered Edward and Viv would be completely inappropriate, even counterproductive, to an adult learner. So he worked until four or so, they had dinner together, watched movies and fucked. Then Michael took the tube home. Except on Friday, when they fucked midafternoon, because at four o'clock Michael was due to head back to Brixton for the weekend.

"Maybe I'll come out there and take a walk round the park," James teased.

"Please don't. God only knows how many other repressed family men stalk that place at night."

"Not sure you really qualify as repressed anymore." James lifted onto his toes to kiss Michael's lips. His normally pale skin was still rosy with a post-orgasm flush. Seeing it made Michael want to tear off his clothes and steer James right back to the bedroom. But Frannie seemed increasingly suspicious. If Michael didn't turn up for dinner on time, there was sure to be a confrontation.

Michael arrived home in a good mood, sat down in the kitchen to await his supper and achieved a state of irritation in less than five minutes. Frannie always wanted him to sit down at the table and listen to her daily monologue – terrible queues at the grocer's, outrageous things her friends said, upcoming TV programs she was sure to enjoy. The kids were also required to be present, at least within earshot in the living room.

Edward was sprawled on the sofa texting a mate. He looked more like Michael with every passing year. There were even glimmers of ginger in Edward's hair, though his adoring mother pretended not to notice. Pretty Viv was on the computer, her attention wavering between Facebook and the telly.

"I feel sorry for Freddie and Sharon. He's retired

now and doesn't know what to do with himself," Frannie said, giving the sauce a taste. "And Sharon's finally found a good GP to help with the fibromyalgia and the chronic fatigue. She wants to get back in the game and enjoy her grandchildren."

"She has no grandchildren," Michael said.

Frannie shot him a look. "Oh, for heaven's sake, Sharon's been married to Freddie for almost thirty years. You're just being pedantic."

"Sharon is no relation to me, Edward or Viv." Michael fought to keep his voice level, especially since the kids were listening. "We've talked about this, Frannie."

"She's your father's wife. Whatever grudges you've held against her since childhood, it's high time you gave them up. I still can't believe you didn't invite them to our wedding or send birth announcements when the kids were born. If Sharon hadn't found me online, I suppose the estrangement would have gone on forever, and it's ridiculous. I'm tired of making excuses for why we never ask them round."

"No need for excuses. Tell them I said they're not welcome."

Frannie took the sauce off the cooker and dumped the pasta in a colander. "I've been a good little peacemaker for a long time, picking out Christmas and birthday cards and signing your name, but I'm done. Sharon's quite nice and mad to get you and your father talking again. So I took the first step. I went round to see them today."

The same sensation Michael felt in Peter's office was rising against, faster and wider in scope. He couldn't locate the words to answer.

Frannie transferred the pasta into a bowl and carried it to the table. Four places were already set with the Maguires' second-best china and silver. The crystal water glasses gleamed. Sometimes Frannie had wine and the kids had milk, but Michael always drank plain water.

"Freddie didn't have much to say. Just sat in a chair working his crossword, nodding and smiling. But he's quite the gardener. I went out back to admire," Frannie said, pouring the sauce into a separate bowl as the oven timer dinged. "There's the bread." She drew out two halves of a French loaf, each covered with melted butter and garlic. "But Sharon talked and talked like she was starved for attention. Made a fuss over Viv's lovely blonde hair."

Michael had been staring at his distorted face in the water glass, thinking he looked like an alien, a bad imitation of a human being. Suddenly he turned in his chair, reflection forgotten. "You took the kids?"

"Of course." Frannie shot him another look. "That was really the point, wasn't it? Viv! Our visit was nice, wasn't it? You liked Gran and Grandpa, didn't you?"

Viv shrugged, flashed a smile and went back to Facebook.

"I didn't like them," Edward said, not looking up from his phone.

Something inside Michael stopped. He felt nothing, or everything. He had no idea which. "Why?" he asked.

"I suppose the old man's okay." Edward's green eyes flicked up to meet Michael's. "But Sharon's weird."

Something Different

During dinner Frannie attempted to drive the conversation like she always did, raising topics and calling on each of them by name to comment. This time, Michael ignored her so pointedly she became flustered. The kids gave one another quick glances and the meal finished in absolute silence.

Michael was sitting on Edward's bed when the boy finished his pre-bedtime shower. One towel slung around his narrow hips and another over his shoulders, Edward entered humming and almost jumped out of his towel when he saw Michael.

"Christ! Dad! Little warning next time!"

"Sorry." Michael stood up. "I don't mean to ambush you. But I need to ask you something, and you have to tell me the truth. The absolute truth." He paused, holding Edward's gaze, trying to drill that imperative into his son's head. "You called Sharon weird. Why?"

Edward grimaced. "I asked her where the loo was. She told me. I went in for a piss and she walked in while I was finishing. I mean, there was no lock on the door, but she knew I was in there." Edward shook his head. "And anyone else would have been all, blimey, sorry love, and ducked out again, but she stayed right there as I turned my back and zipped up. Then she said …" He stopped.

"Said what?"

Edward rolled his eyes. "Said I was big for my age. It was just weird. Maybe I should take it as a compliment. Maybe most guys would like to be told —"

"No," Michael said. "It wasn't a compliment. And most guys would feel exactly the way you did. Revolted." Michael thought he was completely calm, well controlled, but he must have hit a false note because his son placed gentle fingers on his forearm.

"Dad. I'm okay. I just don't want to visit her again."

"You won't have to. I promise." Impulsively Michael gathered Edward in his arms and held him tight. "If anyone ever tries to hurt you, you have to tell me. Right away. Don't wait."

"I know." Edward pulled back. "But, Dad. Are you sure you're okay?"

"Fine." Michael forced his mouth into an approximation of a smile. Then he went to his office, locked the door and ignored Frannie until she went away for the night.

Michael never really slept that night, just dozed. Usually he refused to let his thoughts track backward, but after what Edward had told him, resisting the memories was impossible.

Michael's father, Freddie Maguire, had married Sharon when Michael was six. From the start Michael found his stepmother both mentally and physically intimidating. Freddie was rather short, only five six, and slim as a whip. He had a thing for taller women – Michael's mum had been almost six feet tall – and Sharon, at six one, was right up Freddie's alley. She was huge, not so much fat as massive – broad shoulders, thick arms, thighs like tree trunks. Her voice was deep, her laugh obnoxious, her gaze sharp and knowing.

Even in his preteen years, Michael feared Sharon. Often she drank too much and hounded Freddie from morning to night. But every so often she trundled down to the Baptist church, got saved and cleared the house of alcohol, trashy novels and pulp magazines. Michael rather liked Sharon's religious stretches, even if he found himself rousted out of bed each Sunday morning. When Sharon was right with the Lord, she rarely cursed and never hit. She even had her fags outside on the porch, since she and the Lord had yet to occupy the same page when it came to nicotine. All in all, her religious periods were pleasant intervals until the day she caught thirteen-year-old Michael hunched over the toilet, masturbating.

"I knew it!" Sharon had put on a show of disgust, but those sharp eyes, always rimmed in pale blue eyeliner, had gleamed with a different emotion. Michael hadn't even paused to zip up. He'd just pushed past her, fled to his room and locked the door. Sharon had pounded on it, promising dire consequences if Michael didn't let her in, but he'd stayed in bed with a pillow over his face, wondering if she'd been listening at the bathroom door. She'd burst in just as he ejaculated. Humiliated to the marrow, Michael had wept quietly, unable to imagine anything worse.

Next day, he'd come home from school to find all the locks off the house's inner doors. Sharon had gone round with a screwdriver and removed them all. Except for his bedroom. In that case, the door itself was gone. She'd taken it off its hinges.

Michael, by then accustomed to Sharon's scorched-earth approach, wasn't surprised to also find three church pamphlets on his bed. One was about God's plan for human sexuality. Another was about using prayer to overcome bad habits. The last was a story about a boy who masturbated so much he fell into drink, drugs, free love and suicide. It ended with the boy burning in Hell, which even thirteen-year-old Michael found an excessive punishment for wanking.

After catching him masturbating, Sharon began making unannounced loo inspections. Twice she peeked in through the shower curtain and almost startled him to death. Another time she surprised him while he was sitting on the toilet. Michael started planning his showers around her favorite TV shows. He relied on public toilets whenever possible. At first he'd been relieved, almost grateful, that Sharon hadn't told Freddie about what she'd seen. Then, gradually, Michael began wishing his quiet, peace-loving father would take his eyes off the crossword long enough to notice Sharon's harassment. Michael's father was demonstrative to him in ways Sharon derided, quick with a hug for Michael or a kiss on the forehead. Freddie put on his best suit for all of Michael's school events, clapping loudest when Michael earned a ribbon or certificate. Every goodbye ended with, "Love you, son." Yet when it came to Sharon's new obsession with Michael, Freddie seemed completely unaware.

Finally Sharon's walk with the Lord once again went on hiatus. Crown Royal reappeared in the kitchen. Fags were smoked indoors. She dragged in a pile of well-thumbed paperback romances and read one a day.

Then one night Michael woke to find Sharon sitting

beside him on his bed.

"You're so big for your age," she said. "Bigger than your dad. That's why you can't keep your hands off it. You have a man's cock."

Rooting around under the covers, she'd found his shorts and yanked them down, exposing him. Michael had cried out and Sharon slapped him so hard he saw lights.

"You have no door. Your father is just down the hall," she whispered in Michael's ear, smelling of her favorite combination: Crown Royal and Coca-Cola. "If you wake him and he sees this, it will kill him. Do you want to kill your old dad?"

Too shocked to cry, Michael had shaken his head. When Sharon started stroking him, he pressed his hand in his mouth and closed his eyes. It was over in a few seconds – the humiliation was almost unbearable, she'd seen him come twice now – but to his surprise she started stroking him again, and before long he was as hard as before.

After awhile she stopped. Daring to open his eyes, Michael saw Sharon pull off her top and unfasten her white bra. Her breasts were huge, torpedo-shaped, nipples pointing at her waist. Then off came the rest of her clothes. Beneath the roles of belly fat her vulva was thick with dark hair. Michael closed his eyes again, sure this was only a nightmare, that it couldn't be happening. When her vagina enveloped him, he bit his hand again. That was the worst part, how good it felt, even if seeing her naked made him want to vomit. She rocked a little and he couldn't stop himself from coming inside her.

"And that, little boy, is how men fuck," she'd slurred,

kissing him and wiping away his tears.

It went on like that, on and off, for three years. When Sharon was right with the Lord, she didn't visit him, though she still monitored his loo activities closely. When she and the Lord were at odds, Michael never knew when he'd wake to find Sharon naked and wet with anticipation. Skinny as he was, she continued to overpower him easily even when he finally equaled her in height. It always happened the same way. She stroked him till he was hard, then rode him. Sometimes she kissed him afterward, which he hated more than anything. Quite often it led to slaps because he wouldn't kiss back.

"Don't play coy," Sharon huffed, infuriated. "If you didn't enjoy it, you wouldn't come off like a firecracker every time. You want it worse than I do. Men can't be raped. Their peckers only pop up when they're game."

He'd tortured himself wondering if she were right. He hated her, he hated the visits, he hated himself for coming. Yet from a purely physical standpoint, being ridden by Sharon always brought on orgasm. One night she was bobbing up and down, lips pressed together even as Michael stifled an involuntary moan with his hand. As his gaze shifted from the cracked ceiling to the doorway, he saw his father standing there, watching.

"Dad!" Michael had cried. He should have been ashamed to the bone. Instead he went half-crazed with relief. Freddie had noticed, he'd finally noticed, after all this time he'd cottoned on at last …

Cursing, Sharon had dismounted and gone to her husband. Michael heard raised voices behind their bedroom door, then silence. He lay awake for the rest of the night, wondering if he should get his things together. Would he and his dad be the ones to go, or would Sharon be sent packing? But when dawn came, Sharon cooked bacon and eggs and the three of them ate in silence. Sharon smoked and stared into space. Freddie was deep in another crossword puzzle.

"Love you, son," he called as Michael headed off to school.

It was a few days before Michael cornered his father alone. By then Sharon had visited him twice more, leaving purple bruises on his arms in the process.

"You know what she's doing. Why won't you stop her?"

Freddie had looked sad. "I don't blame you, son. Boys have needs. Sometimes things just happen."

Michael caught his breath. "She - she told you I wanted it? That I—" He tried to say "seduced her," but the phrase was so monstrous, so disgusting, he couldn't force it out. It was the first time Michael, good with words and naturally gregarious, had ever found himself unable to say what he meant.

"I've told you, it's all right. One of those things." Freddie tried to pat Michael's shoulder, grimacing when he jerked away.

"Dad. I want her to stop. Please. Help me. Make her stop."

"Sharon's always had a strong will. Mind of her own," Freddie said, gaze snaking away. "If you don't want to … just say so. Tell her. Or keep on with it, it doesn't matter to me. I still love you, son."

Michael had stared at Freddie. "Why - why do you always say that? Say you love me?"

Freddie blinked. "Boys need a bit of gentleness."

"But if you loved me, you'd help me. You'd make her stop."

Freddie shook his head. "The house is in her name. And I'm too old to start over alone, Michael. Besides, she's my wife. Till death do us part, I take that vow seriously. God's law, not mine …"

Freddie had said more, much more, heaping on words like "son" and "proud" and "love," but Michael realized they were all meaningless – ceremonial, like "thank you" from a bored supermarket clerk. Meant to make him feel good in the short run while signifying nothing at all.

After that Michael had stayed late every day after school. He took up running, then wrestling, then weightlifting. Sharon, back to walking with the Lord, noticed Michael's new physique one warm spring night and promptly went out for a bottle of Crown Royal. But when she turned up in his room, Michael sprang out of bed, caught both her hands and pushed her against the wall.

"You will never touch me again," he said between his teeth, eyes level with hers.

"Let go or I'll scream," she'd cried, trying to break free. She couldn't. She was pure mass; he was strong now, strong and determined.

Backing away, Michael had watched her flee back to the bedroom she shared with Freddie. And just like that, Sharon never visited him again. The swiftness of her capitulation had troubled seventeen-year-old Michael to no end. Had he really wanted it all along? If not, why hadn't he started working out and learning to protect himself sooner? Why hadn't he guessed a bully like Sharon would be terrified by the prospect of real violence?

Not long after Michael had found a roommate through the small ads, moved out, gone away to university and tried to forget. He'd never seen Freddie or Sharon since the day he'd moved out, though he knew they still lived in the same house. It was only twenty kilometers from Brixton.

Around seven the next morning, Michael got into the 4x4, still dressed in his clothes from the night before. He had no idea what he would say when he got to Freddie and Sharon's. But he would say something.

The house looked smaller than he remembered, sagging like a pensioner. But the front garden was neatly kept, shrubs trimmed back for the oncoming winter. The picket fence looked freshly painted.

The hollow gnome was right where it always sat, beneath the water tap. Removing its hidden house key, Michael unlocked the front door and walked inside. Freddie wasn't there. Sharon was sitting on the sofa, smoking a cigarette and watching a morning chat show. Far bulkier than Michael remembered, she got to her feet unsteadily, eyes wide.

"Who the fuck are—" She stopped. "Jesus. It's you. Michael."

He took Sharon in. Older and fatter, she'd let her hair go white. She wore a chenille robe over her housedress and fuzzy pink slippers on her size twelve feet. But her eyes were just the same, sharp and ringed with blue liner.

"My son Edward," he began, finding it difficult to speak. "He told me you surprised him in the loo. Told me what you said to him."

She put her cigarette to her lips. "Never said nothing. He's a dirty little liar. He—"

Michael hit Sharon in the face as hard as he could. She fell back over the sofa, taking it with her as lamps, tables and porcelain knickknacks went everywhere. When Michael came around the other side of the sofa, he found Sharon on her back, nose pouring blood. Drawing back his leg, he kicked her twice. The first time she only grunted. The second time she begged him not to do it again. Her mouth was a red ruin, front teeth snapped in half.

James, Michael thought, returning from someplace far away. *If I kill her, I might never see James again.*

After that he had a choice. He was about to cross a line, from temporary madness to calm decision. Whatever more he did to Sharon after coming back to himself would be on his own head, just as her actions rested on hers.

"Come near my kids again and I'll kill you." He went back to the 4x4 as fast as he could walk. Two streets over he had to stop and vomit up a mouthful of bile. But he didn't feel ashamed. He didn't know what he felt.

James awakened that Saturday morning with nothing to do. By noon he'd finished his weekend homework. Even written a few sentences in his journal, a wide-ruled composition book. His tutor, Ms. Kakowski, said he should write in the journal each day. Sentence structure and spelling didn't matter; at this point, she wouldn't be checking. The point was to get comfortable creating words. James, who'd astonished himself by testing a little ahead of his group – he knew the alphabet in its proper order and could write all the letters – had stared at the blank paper for a long time before daring his first entry. Just a few days ago he'd come across Michael doing the same thing, staring at a blank digital page on the screen of his MacBook. The sight had been oddly encouraging to James. Even smart, bookish, highly literate types occasionally had to face blank whiteness and make a decision.

James's first entry played to his strengths:
MILK FRSOSTED FLAKS
Next day, he checked his spelling against the cereal box and realized he'd missed the mark. Undeterred, his second entry was more ambitious:
ID LIKE MILK WIT FROSTEDFLAKES
Pleased with himself, he'd added his secret weapon, mastered long ago:
JAMES MITCHELL CAMPBELL
He'd never succeeded in making his name look very

fancy, but the letters were all there, and in the correct order, too.

For a long time he'd studied the entry, delighted, before hiding it under the mattress of his twin bed. He wasn't ready for Michael to see his efforts. Not until they were better, until even a man who wrote books for a living would have to concede the words were top-drawer.

It would be a long weekend with Michael gone and his homework finished. James was surprised by how readily he'd taken to the adult literacy program. As a child in school, it had all been about clever vs. stupid, winners vs. losers. Pegged as stupid from age eight, James had never been able to overcome the label, and by age twelve he'd been "Pretty Jamie" and "Poufie Jamie" to boot. But in the adult literacy program, no one thought him stupid or clever – he was just a bloke with dyslexia and a hill to climb. Besides, he had motivations he'd never had as a schoolboy. The world was full of forms, signature lines, websites and text messages. Even something as basic as getting a council flat, not to mention a dole check, required forms, signatures and an e-mail address. Only by learning to read and write would James ever qualify.

Or I could be really ambitious, he told himself, sliding into fantasyland with a guilty little shiver. *I could apply to The Open University. Take classes. Pick a trade and earn my own way.*

He wondered how Michael would feel about that. For that matter, James wondered what anyone might call their current arrangement. James lived in the Shepherd's Bush flat yet did nothing to pay his way, unless cooking counted. He could pretend he earned his keep by fucking Michael, but that wasn't true. Michael would demand James work the tills in a supermarket before he'd insist James fuck him in lieu of rent. That sort of expectation was completely outside the character of a man who'd given James his own bed and even installed a deadbolt on his bedroom door.

Besides, James enjoyed fucking Michael, and that made it mutual fun instead of business. Since that time on the sofa, James had no trouble coming – the door was open, all he needed was sufficient stimulation to pass through. During his five years on the game, James had grown comfortable with other clients. But Michael was more than just a client, and they had passed beyond mere comfort ...

James was watching music videos and wondering if his discontent with the entire Top Forty signaled the advent of old age when his mobile rang. It was Kevin.

"So where you been? Rumor round the Hitching Post is you're dead." Kevin paused. "You dead, mate? That it?"

"Fucking dead," James agreed, heart speeding up. He couldn't help himself; just the sound of Kevin's voice was a tonic to both soul and cock. The night he'd drunkenly made out with Kevin, James had been too emotionally overwhelmed to offer more than a weak hard-on. But whenever he heard Kevin's voice on the mobile, James's cock leapt to attention, vibrating with hope. "What about you? Thought you were poking Silas's ass." Silas was Cunt-Boyfriend's real name.

"Oh, he buggered off, didn't he?" Kevin sounded unconcerned. "Low-rent tosser. I says to meself, Kev, love, you've got to change your type. Get yourself a pretty little love doll. Rosy cheeks and rosy ass and a sweet mouth to suck my cock."

James tried not to take the flattery too much to heart. Kevin had said this sort of thing before, always when fresh off a breakup, when the attentions of a lovely young man seemed especially needful. Yet he'd never done more than cup James's ass in his hands and rub up against him on the dance floor. Kevin liked tall, hard-bodied, silent types who communicated mostly with their tree-trunk cocks. James suspected he was nothing but a cupcake to Kevin, a pretty frosted mouthful to a man who craved red meat.

"So. The Hitching Post. Full of zombies already and due to get worse after dark. Planning to take your dead ass out here? Might manage to liven it up," Kevin said, managing to sound seductive and bored all at the same time.

"Hang on. Get your story straight. Is my ass dead or rosy?"

"It's dead now. It'll be rosy within five meters of me."

James snorted. He'd been in love with Kevin Darden since he was eighteen. And when James was twenty, Kevin had finally stopped thinking of him as a puppy and actually begun paying attention to him. One night they'd killed a bottle of Bacardi and kissed until Kevin unzipped, pulled it out and beat off while sucking James's neck. By then James had been limp – his usual problem, an inability to seal the deal with an unfamiliar partner – but Kev never seemed to notice. James had yet to decide if that meant Kev was extraordinarily polite, refusing to draw attention to an awkward truth, or just extraordinarily self-absorbed.

"I'll be there," James said. Only after he disconnected did he remember he was missing four front teeth.

The Hitching Post was meant to evoke American westerns from the 1940s through the late 1960s. Pictures of John Wayne dotted the walls – from *Stagecoach* to *True Grit* – as well as other American cowboys like Gene Autry, Clint Eastwood, and Roy Rogers. Even iconic horses like Trigger, Silver and Scout had their own framed photos. But the only pictured female was Dale Evans, and her wall was favored by drag queens and rent boys like James. He took his usual place there that Saturday night, beneath a picture of Dale in a sweet pink neckerchief, faithful steed Buttermilk at her side.

James was drinking a bit of coconut rum drowned in Diet Coke. Not much of a cocktail, but when it came to alcohol, he was a featherweight. Recalling the day of the clinic visit, James still couldn't believe he'd downed three premium margaritas and somehow made it to the loo before puking all over Michael's shoes.

If I had, Michael would have wiped it up. Made one of his dry little comments about the incidence of vomiting in Great Britain since WWII ... The imagined commentary made James smile. Michael could find a turd in a punchbowl and say something encouraging. It was just how he was.

"Who's that smile for? Me?" A familiar voice asked.

"'Course it is," James said, replying from his rent boy script. "Cool your heels and let me look at you."

That last bit wasn't a pure line. Kevin wasn't conventionally handsome, but James wasn't caught up in the conventional. He loved Kevin's sharp eyes, his firm mouth, his way of strutting about although he topped James by barely an inch. Like his dad before him, Kevin carried him own cue to the tables, playing billiards and pool with his own stick. He was a master at darts and so good at kissing, half the straight girls never guessed he was queer as a hairy-lipped maiden aunt. Through the week Kevin drove a truck and at nights he shared the bed of a physically dominant man, big in more than mere hands' breadth. James respected this need in Kevin, but he couldn't understand it. Kevin's boyfriends always cheated, always lied and seemed chromosomally incapable of tenderness. When Kevin turned on the charm, entire barrooms fell in love with him. He could have his pick. Yet he always picked the man guaranteed never to give two shits.

"You look a bit banged up." Kevin frowned at James's fading bruises. "Here I've been bragging to everyone about the pretty baby who likes to watch me shoot pool."

James smiled, keeping his lips tightly together. That was probably true. Kevin loved an audience, especially between boyfriends.

"Heard you finally moved out of that hellhole. Where you at these days?"

"Shepherd's Bush," James said with a smile.

"Christ almighty!" Kevin half-rose to his feet. "What the fuck happened to your mouth?"

"Got knocked about, didn't I?" James let his gaze drift around the room. A handwritten sign said POOL, he got that clearly, then some other words harder to work out. Probably there would be a tournament later tonight. He looked back at Kevin. Judging by the other man's expression, James would not be permitted to hang off his arm or kiss the tip of his cue for good luck.

"Oh, don't piss yourself, it's just a few teeth. Getting fixed up in a couple of days. Implants. Be as good as new."

"Implants?" Kevin smiled, trying to regain a bit of his usual *maybe-I-want-you* vibe. "Surprised the NHS would spring for that."

"They aren't. A client is."

Kevin's eyes narrowed. That was his best weapon, his apparent jealousy whenever James mentioned another man. "And you're living with him in Shepherd's Bush?"

James nodded.

"Day in and day out? Keeps you close?" Kevin took a pull off his beer. "Must be sick. Twisted."

"Very twisted. Makes me sleep in a room smaller than Harry Potter's cupboard under the stairs. Mentioned filleting me." Deliberately, James smiled bigger. Kevin flinched. "So what's the story? Finally want to give it a go now that Silas scarpered? I've told you how I feel."

"I'm not ..." Kevin gave one of his dramatic pauses, as if his inner workings were so complex he could barely express himself. "I'm not quite there. Not about anyone. I want to feel that way, you know I do, but it's complicated."

James took a sip of his drink.

"And there's this bloke ..."

James set the drink down.

"His name is Casey. He's a bit – adventurous," Kevin went on. "Likes to mix it up with guest stars, if you get me. I've only seen him once, and he's not into the one-on-one. I told him that's all I ever do. Then I thought ..." Kevin's voice dropped, low, sexy, as his gaze locked with James's. "I thought of you. If it's down to three in a bed, it has to be you. After ..." Kevin pointed at James's mouth. "After you get fixed up, of course."

"Of course." James pressed his lips together.

"Come on," Kevin urged. "You know it'll be good."

"Can't wait. Can't fucking wait," James said, grinning again. "Ring you up soon as the implants are in. Casey won't mind about the herpes, right?"

"What?"

"Genital herpes. I have it. I know you won't care, Kev, but you might mention it to Casey. Good karma to be courteous."

Kevin stared at James. It was the first time James had ever seen the other man speechless.

"Don't fret, love," James said, finishing his drink and standing up. "It'll be the making of me. Gonna sell my story to BBC1. Call it *James Campbell, The Only Man in Britain with Genital Herpes*."

"How's that?" a man at the bar called.

"I said I'm the only bloke in Britain with genital herpes!" James shouted. Kevin was looking at the wall, but a group of girls in the back burst into applause and whistles.

"Don't you believe it!" one of them called as James went out waving and blowing kisses. Maybe his face was bollixed up at present, but the rest of him was nothing to sneeze at.

Back at the flat he pulled out his journal, got a pencil and wrote a variation of something he'd seen on walls, toilet stalls and the tube.

PISS OFF KEV

Two entries in one day. He was becoming – what was Michael's word? Prolific. Pleased with himself, James slipped the journal back into its hiding place and flopped in front of the telly to search for porn.

Michael spent the rest of that Saturday waiting for police cars to pull up alongside the family car, for uniformed officers to knock at the front door, spare Edward and Viv a pitying look and take their father into custody. But the morning passed quietly. So did the afternoon. Frannie demanded an explanation for his behavior the previous night and he promised her she'd have it.

"It's just …" Michael stopped, gathering himself while Frannie peered at him suspiciously. "I hate Sharon. I have my reasons. They will not be put aside. And I will not have my children around that woman."

Frannie, who'd never heard Michael speak about anything with such an obvious underpinning of emotion, agreed to defer the discussion. Dinner passed more or less normally, still without knuckles rapping at the door. Then, ignoring three curious stares, Michael poured himself a glass of Frannie's Chardonnay and went up to his office.

The blank digital page taunted him for a while, but the wine helped. The fact he'd admitted aloud that he hated Sharon helped, too. And the memory of striking her helped most of all. It took Michael, author extraordinaire of all things simple, unadorned and purely factual, four hours to type up his narrative. In the end it was coldly clinical and less than two pages long. But it would explain to Frannie exactly why he felt the way he did, should he ever gather the courage to let her read it.

The next day he woke and skipped the shower. He wasn't pleasuring himself that way anymore; he was saving all his sexual energy for James. It crossed his mind that James might be up to absolutely anything that weekend. Working, if he dared try it despite the missing teeth. Partying with friends. Fucking some other man. All three ideas hurt to imagine. But Michael was firm in his resolution that he was no longer buying James. Even if James left him tomorrow, Michael had no intention of giving up his peaceful little flat in Shepherd's Bush. He could afford it, he didn't need a roommate, didn't feel cheated by paying the water and gas bills while James took classes. As long as James wanted to stay, Michael would welcome him, gladly.

Most of his clothes needed a wash. Pulling on one of

Edward's T-shirts – a size too small, but not unbearable – and an old pair of jeans, Michael went out to the back garden and started cleaning dead annuals from the raised beds. His right hand was sore and swollen across the knuckles, so he put on gardening gloves. Either Sharon was too terrorized from the beating to identify her attacker or Freddie was too passive to call the police on his son, just as he'd been unwilling to stand up to his wife. Michael no longer feared arrest. But still, it was prudent to work with his hands out in the open today, creating a plausible reason for the bruising in case he was asked to explain …

By early afternoon Michael had shifted to the front garden, giving the lawn one final cut before autumn turned to winter. Edward's T-shirt was too tight through the biceps and shoulders, so finally Michael pulled it off, finishing the lawn bare-chested. He was raking up grass clippings when Lisa popped round to introduce herself.

Lisa was in her late twenties, recently divorced and new to the neighborhood. She pointed out the house she'd moved into, a serviceable three-bedroom with no front garden to speak of. Since Michael was clearly an expert on the subject, not to mention a neighbor, Lisa wanted to hear his opinion on pampas grass. Was it done to death? Would purple fountain grass be better? Would a small stand of bamboo be completely mad?

Michael, author of *Gardening for Beginners*, gave Lisa several opinions and pointers. It wasn't until her eyes raked over his bare chest for the third time that he realized he was being chatted up. He couldn't pretend not to be pleased. Only when Frannie marched outside on some wafer-thin pretext and introduced herself did Lisa's enthusiasm waver.

"Cow," Frannie muttered at Lisa's departing back.

"I'm done here," Michael said mildly. "Think I'll have a shower."

When he emerged, entering the master bedroom in his terry-cloth robe, Frannie was nude on the bed. Her legs were spread, showing off the waxed landing strip she maintained so carefully. "Michael. Come here. Don't tell me you don't want it."

Michael let his breath out. Lisa's interest had flattered him. Imagining that porn scenario James had teased him with – the pair of them sharing a willing female, Michael in the front door, James in the back, striving toward each other as Lisa cried out in pleasure – had given him an erection. But he was saving it for James, for the fun they'd have first thing tomorrow morning, even before breakfast …

He sat down beside Frannie. She was already undoing his belt, opening his robe. "Oh, yes," she murmured at the sight of him, just as she had during their courtship.

He pushed her onto her back, willing to try once more, to see if anything remained. She was kissing him wildly, probably fantasizing about one of her telly actors, tugging on his cock with a firm hand. It felt good. And pushing inside her would feel good, for him at least, even if he never managed to please her. And if he begged off, there'd be hell to pay. Obviously the sight of Lisa eyeing her husband had been too much for Frannie, had stoked her territorial instincts and goaded her to this desperate act …

"Frannie," he whispered, pulling back. "Just a second. Give me a second …"

He found his trousers from the day before, right where he'd left them draped atop the clothes bin. Locating his wallet, he opened it and returned to the bed with a square foil packet in hand.

"If we're going to do this," he said, holding up the condom and meeting her eyes, "we'll need one of these."

Frannie stared at him. Then she sighed, deflating from her randy housewife persona to her true self. Rising, she crossed to the hook behind the door, finding her pink silk robe and belting it tight. "So whatever's going on, it's not just an emotional affair. You're fucking her."

Michael didn't answer.

"How long?" Frannie asked. She was perfectly composed, more brittle than angry.

"A month or so."

"Is it a fling? Something you had to get out of your system?"

Michael shook his head.

Frannie tried to laugh, but he saw the hurt and fear in her eyes. "Are you telling me that it's some grand passion? That it's love?"

"It is for me," Michael said. "I'm not sure how he feels."

Frannie caught her breath. "It's – it's a man?"

Michael nodded.

Frannie put her hands over her face. "Why are you doing this?" she whispered through her fingers.

Michael waited until she peeked through. "It started

as sex. I didn't mean for things to go this far. I only wanted something different. To feel something." Speaking the truth to Frannie was painful, but he knew he owed it to her, even if she hated him for it, even if he burned in cartoon Baptist Hell like the masturbating boy from Sharon's pamphlet. "But it became a friendship. Then I fell in love."

"So – you're gay now? That's what you're saying?"

"I haven't quite worked out what I am. It doesn't matter. I want a divorce. I want to be with him."

"So you'll leave me and go shack up with some man? Do you have any idea what that will do to Viv? *To Edward?*" Frannie flung at him, voice breaking.

It was on Michael's tongue to say they hadn't reared their children to be homophobic, to judge anyone by whom that person loved, but then he saw Frannie was shaking all over. She was terrified, invoking any name that might give him pause.

"Frannie. Tell me the truth," he said gently. "Do you love me?"

She made a soft sound, almost a sob. "Little hard right now."

"Before I came out of the shower. When you were waiting for me on the bed. Did you love me?"

"God knows I've tried."

"Frannie."

"No!" she cried suddenly, staring at him with that familiar fire in her sharp blue eyes. This was the woman who had quite a lot to say when he failed to put out the rubbish bins or deleted one of her unwatched telly programs. "No, but did you love me?"

He shook his head slowly.

"Oh, Christ," Frannie whispered. She passed a hand over her face, regarding him with dry eyes. "This is really happening, isn't it? I'm not dreaming."

Michael scooted a little closer. "What frightens you so much about divorcing me?"

She crossed her arms over her chest and looked away.

"Tell me. We aren't in love. We don't enjoy spending time together. I know you love the kids and I'd never try to separate you from them. You're their mum, they adore you and you adore them. You can't be afraid I'd muck about on that score."

"They need a father."

"They'll have one. Probably a better one, now that I'm pulling my head out of my ass." He smiled at her astonished look. "Sorry. Lately my vocabulary has – expanded. I know you love this house, you enjoy your life the way it is, the spin classes, the book club …"

Frannie's eyes widened. "So I'm a mercenary, is that it? Sticking with you so I won't have to go back to a council flat and ring up sales at Boots for a living?"

"Maybe." Michael didn't quite dare touch her, so he leaned closer instead. "I wouldn't want a divorce if it meant going back to a place like the one you grew up in. It was hell there, wasn't it?"

Frannie nodded.

"If it meant being forced to take a job like that, or losing everything that makes you happy, I wouldn't blame you for being afraid," Michael continued. "But a divorce doesn't have to be adversarial. I assumed you and the kids would prefer to stay here. I'll never take this house away from you, Frannie. God knows it's yours – you're the one who made it a home. Besides, I already have a flat in the city. I could take the tube in, visit the kids on weekends."

Frannie appeared to consider that. "But I'll be divorced. A divorced woman at thirty-three. Old, fat, past my prime. Used up."

Michael squelched the smile that threatened. Frannie's lament reminded him of nothing so much as James declaring himself a dirty, diseased whore. Probably it was romantic obsession – Michael was so in love with James, he saw his imprint everywhere. Otherwise this was surely a sign that in some alternate universe James and Frannie were the best of friends, giggling over magazines and giving each other pedicures.

"Frannie. If you knew you'd snuff it in the next ten years. If you had just ten years of life left. Would you want to spend them married to me? Or would you want to strike out, give it a go, try to find real happiness somewhere else?" Michael touched her cheek at last. "We married young. We had two beautiful children and I'll always be grateful to you for that. I don't want to take anything from you. I just want to move on. Don't you?"

She looked at his red, swollen right hand as if seeing it for the first time. "What happened to you?"

Michael got dressed – he never knew when Viv and one of her preteen friends might appear around a corner – and retrieved his printed narrative from the office. Returning to Frannie still sitting on the bed in her pink silk robe, he held out the pages.

"Edward's fine," he blurted. "You need to know that.

He's completely fine. As for you taking the kids to see Sharon – that was my fault, I know that. I should have told you the truth. I was just too ashamed. But I wrote it out for you."

Mystified by his preamble, Frannie took the pages and began to read.

James woke early on Monday morning. He had everything ready in the fridge – six eggs, grated cheddar cheese, sausages, coffee, butter and cream. Plus a loaf of sliced oat bread on the counter, ready for toasting. The only question in James's mind was, would he fuck Michael the moment he came through the door? Or feed him breakfast first, then fuck him?

But Michael didn't turn up at 7:30, or 8, or 8:30. James was just starting to imagine disaster scenarios – derailed trains, terrorist bombings, Michael collapsing with a heart attack and dying on route to hospital – when his mobile rang. It was Michael.

"How are you?" Michael asked in his habitual tone, gentle with a hint of dry humor.

"Little worried, mate. Where the fuck are you?"

"Something came up at home. I have to deal with it and it won't be quick. So I won't make Shepherd's Bush before midafternoon." Michael paused as if weighing his words even more carefully than usual. "Is everything all right?"

"Fab. Is—" James started to say "wifey," but stopped himself. No more talking to Michael like he was a client. "Is Frannie next to you?"

"Yes. But don't worry. I'll be there as soon as I can."

James tried not to pout after Michael disconnected. But had Michael forgotten what today was? The depth of James's irritation surprised him. By rights he should have been heartbroken over what happened at the Hitching Post, the realization that Kevin only wanted his help securing the interest of another man, but James had already put that aside. His pursuit of Kevin had been a bit like the time James had tried to convince everyone in his study group that the word "knot" was "coat." After finally being made to see the light, Ms. Kakowski said James tended to make rapid assumptions about disconnected words instead of working them out in the context of the sentence. Even if the "k" confused him, he should have guessed the sentence "I can tie a—" wouldn't end with the word coat. It was the same with Kevin. No matter how attractive James found Kevin, he should have guessed a bloke who only went for nonverbal gladiators would never fall in love with a cheeky, chirpy pretty boy.

But Michael not turning up on time ... Michael off and doing God knew what with his wife, something that couldn't wait ... James felt agitated, disappointed, toyed with. Only by taking out a certain memory and examining it - the night Michael begged for his cock - did James manage to soothe himself. During his stint as a professional, James had learned that men said all sorts of things as they ejaculated, including calling for Mum and asking God for forgiveness. And in the post-orgasm halo they promised, flattered and swore devotion. Michael's words – "Of course not, I love you" – probably fell under that category, the noises a man's mouth made when his brain translated, "My cock is happy. Thank you," into something needlessly ornate. Only an idiot took what was said then as real; real was material. Real was concrete.

Real was paying for dental implants and making a second bedroom and installing a deadbolt, James thought, re-examining Michael's words in the context of all that came before. Afterwards he was strangely lighthearted, strangely energetic. And since Michael would be very late, James had a quick breakfast and embarked on his day.

Michael had barely been in the flat for ten minutes when James returned. He had an armful of new books from the Learning Annex. He also carried a composition book that he tucked carefully beneath them, as if it contained top-secret information.

"About time you turned up," James said, sauntering slowly up to Michael with a wide, delighted grin.

"Look at you." Standing up, Michael went to the other man and slid his arms around him. He kissed him on the neck, then pulled back for another look. The implants looked flawless, but James's upper lip had a swollen, bee-stung appearance.

"Paul did a great job. Does your mouth hurt?" Michael asked.

"It would, but I have oxycodone," James said, withdrawing a bottle from his jeans pocket and shaking it at Michael. "Hear that sound? Mating call of Bethnal Green, mate." Still grinning, James slid back into Michael's arms, pressing his head against his chest. Delighted, Michael squeezed back.

"Thank you," James whispered against him.

"You're welcome. So all you have to take is some painkillers?"

"And more antibiotics. And this," James said, going to the kitchen and picking up another plastic prescription bottle. "An antiviral. Saw my GP today. He said if a patient takes one of these daily, quite often the herpes goes to sleep and never wakes up. So I might never have a breakout, and you might never catch it."

Michael nodded. It was the furthest thing from his mind, but James was transparently thrilled with the news, and Michael didn't want to detract from the other man's pleasure. "Are you up for a kiss on the lips?"

James shook his head. "I'm game for anything else, though. Well – except it might be a while before I fellate you."

Michael surprised himself with how heartily he laughed. "Let me guess. You've been issued a dictionary."

"Not one of my own yet," James said, shy and proud and preening all at the same time. "But Ms. Kakowski helps us look up words. I told her I was searching for a really posh term for playing the skin flute. She went to fellate straight away."

"Was she shocked?"

"I'll say. She said everyone else tries to look up blow job. I told her my boyfriend's a writer. Not quite sure she believed me."

Before Michael could quite digest how he felt about casually being referred to as a boyfriend, James caught sight of Michael's suitcase beside the sofa and made a high, delighted chirp. It was the same noise he'd made when Michael revealed he'd booked them a room at the Green Park Hilton.

"Oh my God," James cried, spinning around as if he'd just won the lottery. "You're not going back on the tube tonight, are you? You've come to stay!"

Michael pulled James back into his arms. Mindful of his sore mouth, Michael kissed James's white throat instead, licking and nipping along the line of his jaw. Digging his fingers into James's thick brown hair, Michael let his mouth travel up, tongue working along the soft brown fur of one sideburn. Then he was nibbling James's earlobe, tugging at it, thrusting his tongue in the earhole as James let out a little moan.

"Did you fuck another man this weekend?" Michael whispered. He was hard no matter what the answer was, but he had to know, had to hear the answer.

"No. I saw Kevin. I don't – he's not – he's not you. I left him sitting with his drink and came home again …"

Michael pulled James's T-shirt up over his head and cast it aside. He loved those pink nipples, the way they stood out on that pale chest. Putting his lips to one, he sucked the nipple, feeling it harden against his tongue and then twisting it cruelly.

"Oh!" James undid the top three buttons of his jeans,

opening his fly enough to free the head of his cock.

"If you're not fucking anyone else, and I'm not fucking anyone else, we don't need condoms anymore," Michael said, pressing his hand against James's flat belly. That cock was just beneath his fingertips, straining toward him, but Michael resisted the urge to seize and pull it. "I want to be inside you with nothing between us, nothing but you and me. I want to see my cum drip out your ass."

"Michael …"

Michael worked James's jeans off, then his shorts, overwhelmed as always by the sight of this perfect nude male. "Let me fuck you. Let me fuck you raw, just this once, let me come inside you and make you feel it …"

James made a little sound and Michael, drunk on the moment, sure of himself as he hadn't been sure in years, lifted James in his arms and carried him to the bed. Placing the other man on his back, Michael kicked off his shoes and stripped quickly, tossing down coat, waistcoat, tie, shirt, pants, socks and shorts. It didn't matter what got creased. Cock so hard it hurt, Michael threw a leg over James. The plastic bottle of lube was right where he left it, tucked in the space between mattress and frame. Squirting lubricant over himself, Michael passed the bottle to James, who spread a fair amount between his cheeks, working three fingers into himself and groaning. It was gorgeous, this beautiful young man impaled on his own oiled fingers, spreading his asshole, making soft sounds as he worked himself loose. Then he tossed the bottle aside and gripped Michael's cock so hard it throbbed desperately, guiding the organ down even as James lifted himself.

Entry was hot, delicious, perfect. Aware that the visual could push him over the edge, Michael closed his eyes, focusing on the physical alone. He'd never felt James from within, never really been inside him, and pleasure was so intense Michael kept pushing his way within until James gasped.

"Michael ... please..."

Michael opened his eyes. Leaning forward, he covered James with his own body, kissing the other man's throat again, watching James's Adam's apple ripple with pleasure or pain. Now entirely inside James, Michael began rocking, the gentlest possible lovers' rhythm. James made a little noise.

"You're so big ..."

"Can you take it?" Michael whispered, hips moving a little faster.

"Give it to anyone else and I'll kill you." James kept rising up to meet him, lifting perfectly with Michael's cadence.

"Squeeze me." Michael groaned as James clenched inside, white-hot and tight as a bear trap. Now they were rocking faster, Michael supporting himself on his elbows, James groaning, eyes shut tight. It was the pinkness spreading across James's chest, the trembling in his rock-hard cock, that made Michael come up suddenly, rising to his knees and fucking James with fresh brutality.

"That's it," Michael said as James grimaced, gasping low in his soft white throat. "Take me, take all of me, take me—"

"*Oh*," James cried again, back arching.

"I love you, James," Michael gasped, dealing a final battering thrust. James screamed, his cum hotter than piss against Michael's belly. Then it was Michael's turn, pressing in deep as he could, pumping his cum into James. Time shifted, blurring things between them, putting Michael into another place where there was no need for ego, reassurance or even reciprocity. He felt what he felt for James and took the deepest possible pleasure in it; the emotion was its own reward. Finally when he was completely soft, Michael withdrew, rolling onto his back beside James. He was almost surprised when the other man curled into his arms. But he let himself enjoy it, let himself go half-weak with pleasure. This was sublime, loving, truly loving, and expecting nothing but the freedom to express it.

"Did you leave Frannie?" James whispered, clinging to Michael with his cheek pressed against Michael's chest.

"Yes. We chose a solicitor and started proceedings this morning."

"You didn't – you didn't hit her, did you?"

Michael made a soft sound of amusement. "She's the mother of my children. I'd never hit her. Any more than I'd ever hit you."

"So what happened to your hand?"

Michael wasn't sure how long the silence stretched between them. But finally he realized he had nothing to fear. Then he began to speak.

Within two weeks, James's mouth had fully healed, making his previous regiment of soft foods unbearable. Michael suggested dinner at Gardenia, an East End bistro not far from the London Eye. James protested he had nothing to wear, and Michael was surprised at his own insensitivity. It was true, James had hardly any wardrobe to speak of.

"You can't keep buying me things," James protested as the tailor went off in search of a certain fabric. When he bit his lower lip that way, his eyes looked even wider, even bluer. "After I finish the literacy program and get a job, I'll be hopelessly behind. Never earn enough to pay you back."

"Is that what you think I want?" Michael lifted James's hand, brushing the knuckles with his lips. That had started as a joke between them, a way for Michael to kiss James while his mouth healed, but now it was a private gesture, something they both enjoyed. "To balance my checkbook at some point, even stevens?"

"Things should be equal between us." James turned away from the haberdasher's triple mirror, avoiding his own reflection, handsome though he was in the tacked-up suit pieces.

Michael smiled. Since splitting with Frannie, he'd become a little too frank – more than one person had made the observation. Yet he couldn't stop himself from saying exactly what he meant.

"Things can never be equal between us, not financially. I've had a fund settled on me since I was a little boy. Plus I've made a good living at technical writing. Your family had nothing left over to give you and you haven't been trained for any sort of work."

"Thanks for that," James muttered, suddenly fascinated by the carpet.

"Can you really not understand?" Michael slid his arms around James from behind.

"Too stupid to understand."

"None of that, or I'll tell Ms. Kakowski." James's tutor had challenged him to go seven days without once referring to himself as stupid. So far he was failing miserably. It would take more than a week to shake off the conditioning of a lifetime.

"James." Michael kissed his ear. "I started the game with Mayfair and Park Lane. You started the game with do not pass go, do not collect two hundred pounds. When you and I watch a bit of cinema, we're equal. Sampling wine at a vineyard, we're equal. Fucking," Michael lowered his voice, "seeing which of us can make the other come first, we're equal. But financially – no. So we have two choices. I can hoard my money. Or we can enjoy it together."

"One day you'll resent it," James said stubbornly, biting his lower lip.

"Says who?"

"*Take A Break*," James said, referring to a colorful lowbrow magazine featured prominently in supermarkets. "There was an article on keeping your man. My group read it in class. Well – at lunch. And relying on him for gifts is a sure means of driving him away."

"Want to keep your man?" Michael murmured, so pleased he wondered if they could make it back to Shepherd's Bush without ducking into someplace for a mutual wank. "Let him suit you up and see how gorgeous you are."

By then the little white-haired tailor was back again, cloth in hand and clearing his throat. Michael withdrew to a chair, enjoying the view as James was fitted, measured and fitted again. When the tailor measured James's inseam yet a third time – "Just to be sure" – Michael was tempted to protest. Mild and unassuming as the tailor looked, he was no doubt enjoying every trip up James's inner thigh, each time murmuring, "Dresses to the right …"

The dark blue suit with a faint pinstripe was finished by four o'clock. Their dinner reservations at Gardenia were for seven. Taking the new suit back to Shepherd's Bush, Michael was tempted to spend the interval in bed with James. But no. They'd never once had a proper date – cab, starter, entrée, dessert, kiss and *then* bed. At least once in their relationship, they'd do things conventionally.

So they spread a Scrabble board on the coffee table and played using Ms. Kakowski's rules. No score was kept and all words had to be two, three, or four letters. No penalty was issued for misspellings, but the word had to be corrected before the game went on. Michael offered "tack" and James immediately tried to form "kick" off it, spelling it "kik."

"Left out the letter c," Michael said.

James sighed. "Seriously, who thought up silent

letters? Why include a letter if it's *silent*? Just to fuck with dyslexics?"

The doorbell chimed. Michael got up to answer it and found Germanotti on the front step. He hadn't quite uttered "Come in" before the other man bounded over the threshold.

"So sorry to burst in, you know I'd never interrupt, but there's a problem with—" Eyes ranging around the flat, Germanotti's gaze fell on James. He affected surprise. "Why. Michael. Who's this?"

"You know who he is. Bob Germanotti, this is James Campbell. James, you've heard me mention Germanotti. And he's heard about you. He was with me the night I decided to walk to Brixton Park."

"Bloody hell," Germanotti groaned. "I was trying to be discreet. Now you've made me sound like the asshole friend in *Pretty Woman*." He gave James a reassuring look. "I promise I am not Jason Alexander from *Pretty Woman*."

"No worries, mate," James smiled, coming around the sofa to put out a hand. Germanotti appeared mesmerized, the handshake lasting a beat longer than it should have.

"So what's happening?" James asked. "Textbook stampede? Some sort of word shortage?"

Germanotti giggled girlishly. Michael had to press a hand to his mouth to keep from bursting out laughing.

"Not so much. Just - just trouble with the McGuffin Reader. Wouldn't want to bore you. Michael, could I have a quick word?"

They went out on the front porch, closing the door behind them. Germanotti looked dazed. "Michael."

"Yes?"

"I've gone gay."

"It'll pass."

"Didn't say I wanted it to pass right away." Germanotti sounded mutinous.

"Fine. I give you permission to think of James the next time you sleep with Wendy."

Germanotti perked up. "Really? I had my birthday back in July, but Christmas is only a few weeks away …"

"The McGuffin Reader?" Michael prompted. It was a private gag between them, a nonexistent project referred to when supervisors were listening.

"The entire neighborhood knows about you and James. Lisa – you know, divorced blonde Lisa – came by your place looking for gardening advice and Frannie told her you buggered off to Shepherd's Bush to, well, get buggered. Lisa was devastated, but Frannie seemed fine with the whole thing."

"She is. And I knew already. Frannie rang me up to say so. We'd already told the kids, so she was free to tell anyone else whatever she wanted."

Germanotti, who had two sons of his own, looked pained. "How are Edward and Viv?"

Michael sighed. "Viv isn't doing well. We'll be starting family counseling soon."

"And Edward?"

"He followed me to Shepherd's Bush last Monday. Came up to the flat, had a look round, met James. We talked." Michael left out the details because he didn't want to get emotional, not with a lovely evening at Gardenia just around the corner. It had been a revelation to discover Edward had always viewed Michael as distant, unloving and literally perfect. The episode with Sharon – Michael guessing what happened and taking Edward's side over that of a seemingly responsible adult – had shaken Edward's notion of his father. The divorce and Michael's insistence on admitting everything, including his infidelity and James's prior occupation, had exploded that notion altogether. Edward was shy of James and shell shocked by his mother's growing pleasure in her own independence. It would take time. But Edward had ended the visit by telling Michael he loved him, and Michael, tearing up, had said it back.

"He's a good kid. He'll make it." Germanotti sounded unconvinced.

"He will." Michael smiled, patting the other man's shoulder reassuringly. "But it's good of you to worry. Know what? I don't miss my cubicle, but I've missed you. Come round for drinks tomorrow evening?"

"Thought you'd never ask. Tell James I said cheers," Germanotti said, and headed down the stairs.

Around six o'clock, James allowed Michael to attire him in the day's purchases – black silk socks, creamy silk boxers, white shirt with pearl buttons, brass cufflinks, waistcoat, coat and Italian shoes. They got through the operation with only a kiss or two, then engaged a cab to take them to Gardenia.

The traffic was beastly. The cab would roll forward a few meters, only to halt for two or three minutes at a time. The driver, a middle-aged lady named Amira, made only a few stabs at conversation, falling into tactful silence when James slid into Michael's arms.

"I adore the beard," James said, kissing Michael's ginger-furred cheek. "But tomorrow I'm shaving it off and making you start all over again."

"What about my hair?" It had come in fully. If Michael wanted to keep the Caesar, he'd need to cut it soon.

"Leave it. Let it get even longer," James breathed, climbing into Michael's lap. Michael didn't protest when hands unzipped his trousers and drew him out. He made a soft noise as James rode him a little, the dark navy silk between his cheeks caressing Michael's cock.

"Don't come. Not so much as a drop," James whispered in Michael's ear, "or you'll ruin my new pants."

They made out in the cab's cigarette- and cigar-smelling backseat until Amira called, "Clear sailing now, boys!"

James dismounted; Michael tucked his erect member back into his trousers with effort. Still indecent, Michael pulled off his jacket and put it in his lap. James checked his reflection in the door window and smoothed his hair. From the many times sloe-eyed, smiling Amira glanced in her rearview mirror, she'd been watching the action all along.

"What do I owe you?" Michael asked as Amira pulled up outside Gardenia.

"Just this." She passed him her card with her car number and company ID. "Next time you two need a ride, call me. I've had many couples in my cab, many, many. But none so beautiful as you."

"But … the fare …" Michael spluttered. Amira shook her head, waved at James and pulled away.

At precisely seven o'clock, Gardenia's concierge led Michael and James to a central table draped in white linen. Appearing as if conjured, a waiter poured water into cut-crystal glasses and presented them with menus.

"Tonight," the waiter announced in rich Shakespearean tones, "we offer trout with potato compote. Ham hock terrine with onion marmalade. Crispy chicken breasts with fresh thyme. Risotto with squash and sage."

"The trout," Michael said.

"The crispy chicken breasts," James said.

"I recommend Riesling or Pinot Grigio as an accompaniment," the waiter intoned.

"Water," Michael said.

"Diet Coke," James said.

"Excellent." Making no secret of his disgust, the waiter stalked away.

They sampled the starter, a whole grain loaf spread with tangerine marmalade. James pressed a foot against Michael's leg, stroking him from ankle to knee. Then he took out a pen and pad, another of Ms. Kakowski's requirements. Writing something down, he pushed the paper at Michael.

Your hot.

Michael smiled. Locating his own pen, he wrote back one word: *You're.* James had difficulty with contractions.

James scowled, adding something and pushing the paper back again.

You're a dick.

Michael marked through the full stop. Adding a word, he pushed the paper across the table.

You're a dick magnet.

It took James a second to work out the unfamiliar written word. Then he looked up, grinning. "Am I?"

"Thought I'd have to fight Germanotti for the privilege of taking you out tonight."

Biting his lower lip, James wrote something else. He hesitated, watching Michael for a moment before pushing it over.

Love you.

Michael took a deep breath. He'd known, known for a while, yet it didn't make the declaration any less sweet. He added something.

I Love you more.

James thought for a moment. Finally he added something and returned the napkin.

I Love you more then chikin.

They were still laughing over that when the entrées arrived. The waiter, looking still disgusted by the lack of culinary decorum, set down their plates and drifted off to assist more deserving patrons. Reaching across the table, Michael took James's hand and brushed his lips against the knuckles. That taste of bread had been sufficient. He wasn't hungry for anything else. Anything except James.

"Keep that up and we might get bashed," James murmured, cutting his eyes to the left.

Glancing over, Michael saw a stylish blond couple.

The woman was intent on her wine; the man was glaring at Michael and James. Shrugging, Michael turned back to his trout. It wasn't particularly good; Frannie's cooking was better. James seemed equally unimpressed with his chicken. They both decided to forgo dessert.

"I need a piss before we go," James said.

Michael smiled. "Lead the way."

The men's room was all white tiles, fluorescent lights and gleaming urinals. James headed toward one and Michael stopped him. "Let's take the stall."

James broke into a slow grin. "Right."

The stall was a tight fit for two grown men. To lock the door Michael had to put his back to it while holding James from behind. James pulled out his cock. Taking it in hand, Michael aimed for him, aroused by the stream of bright yellow urine. Then he heard the men's room door open and went even harder. As James finished up, some other man unzipped in front of the nearest urinal and started to piss.

"Shake it gentle," James whispered. "Don't splash my suit."

Michael obeyed, pressing his massive erection against James's ass at the same time.

"Oh, yes," James whispered. "Should've guessed you'd enjoy beginner's water sports."

"I'd enjoy anything with you." Michael released the other man's cock long enough to dig into his wallet and locate a condom. Protection didn't matter, but James would need the lubricant …

As Michael undid his own fly, he heard the men's room door open again. The first patron was using one of the sinks; another was unzipping. Tearing open the foil packet, Michael worked the tight, slippery condom into place. Then he unfastened James's trousers, pushing down his shorts to expose that firm, round ass.

"Bend forward," he whispered. James did so, head level with the tank as he gripped it. Cock poking between James's warm cheeks, Michael pushed in harder than usual. James made a high pained noise that echoed off the white-tiled walls.

Footsteps neared the stall. James looked over his shoulder at Michael. Michael was hot all over, trembling with arousal; James's entire body had turned pink.

Putting a finger to his lips, Michael pressed up his ass even harder, filling James until the other man gasped. He shook the tank so hard the porcelain lid rattled, but despite his pain Michael knew James wanted more. He could tell by the way James kept their bodies together, pushing back instead of sliding forward. Soon Michael found the correct angle. There was no doubt; James transformed from tight all over to supple with pleasure. He began to moan, low in his throat but still audible.

"Oi! Mate! All right in there?" A man rattled the stall's locked door.

Michael heard rapid whispers beside the urinals, then nervous laughter. But he couldn't focus solely on his own exhibitionism; he had to make James come. From the other man's face – mouth clenched, eyes shut tight – it wouldn't happen easily. Ignoring the men outside, the urinals flushing, those soft voices, Michael pulled James upright. He pressed both hands against

James's belly, inducing another, louder cry. Now at maximum penetration, holding James tight so he couldn't break rhythm if he tried, Michael began thrusting up and up, determined and relentless.

"James. Let go," Michael commanded, not caring who heard. Grasping his own cock, James began pulling wildly.

"Let go, James," Michael said again, leaning against the locked door so hard the entire stall shook. "Let go, let g—"

James came with a long, shuddering groan. Michael, who never put his hand in his mouth anymore, emitted his usual cry, probably loud enough to be heard on the dining room floor. It didn't matter. They'd paid through the nose for a substandard dinner. The least Gardenia could offer them was ten minutes of actual pleasure.

When they finally emerged from the stall, decent to face the world and generally composed, the men's room was empty. James rose up on his toes, put his arms around Michael's neck and kissed him gently.

"I really do," he whispered.

"What?"

"Love you. I hope – hope everything turns out okay between you and your kids. I don't want you to lose anything more because of me. Not just money. Anything."

Michael stared at James. It was rather like learning how Edward had viewed him for all those years. The potential for human beings to misunderstand one another was apparently limitless. Michael cupped the other man's face in his hands.

"James. You've never cost me a thing. Everything I have is because of you." Michael kissed his lips. "Now let's go home.

Epilogue

Michael's first attempts at writing fiction were unfortunate. His later ones were more technically proficient but uninvolving. With each story he got a little better, gained a little more confidence, but writing fiction was nothing like constructing a textbook. There were no absolutes in fiction, no certain way to deliver what was needed. So it was no surprise most technical writers considered novel writing a gateway to madness.

Michael's most recent effort had been turned down by every publisher, large and small. The only thing left was to self-publish, as many were doing these days, or let the book languish on his hard drive and start something new. Most of his writer friends advised the latter. Only one advised, "Fuck it. Self-publish." And that was Germanotti, best-selling author of *The Francis Fish Experience*, soon to be a major motion picture.

It turned out that seventeen years of cyber-slacking and phoning it in at the company had given Germanotti sufficient time and material to finish his novel. And a major publishing house had snapped it up, optioning both the TV and cinema rights before the book was a month old. *The Francis Fish Experience* was a comic stream-of-consciousness story narrated by a middle-aged, suburban Englishman. It detailed his cold wife, scheming kids and soulless workplace in humorous yet heartfelt prose. In the course of the novel, Francis's work mate Betty met a tattooed, pierced lesbian, fell in love with her and upended her stale, dissatisfying life. Many readers found Betty's subplot the most affecting part of the novel. Germanotti didn't deny he derived everything in the book from his own life. He even signed Michael's copy with, "To Michael. You'll always be Betty to me."

"I'll never finish this," James complained from the sofa. He was on his tablet, working through his homework from The Open University. He stood to graduate this term, but the workload made him cranky. Plus, their weekend had been torpedoed by Frannie's wedding. It wasn't that they resented the invitation, far from it, but the rehearsal and ceremony had taken half of Friday and all of Saturday.

"Shouldn't have spent so much time on the PlayStation with Edward." Michael peeked to see if the hint had sunk in. It hadn't. The console and controllers remained strewn across the floor. They would stay there until Michael himself put them away.

Then again, he was probably foolish to begrudge a little untidiness. Edward's fondness for James pleased Michael to no end. Viv might never warm up – as the therapist was wont to say, Michael could ask for forgiveness, but he couldn't set a timeline. Four years hadn't been long enough for Viv; maybe forty wouldn't do it. But in fairness, Viv didn't care much for Frannie's husband either, and Louis was charm himself.

Louis Bourg hailed from a village thirty kilometers from Paris. Sixty-two years old and widowed, he operated a highly successful vineyard, putting Michael's pretensions of financial security in the shade. Frannie only went out with Louis that first time because of his wealth. She'd felt certain a short, balding, pot-bellied man could do nothing for her, no matter how much he was worth on paper. But Louis lived, breathed and spoke romance fluently. He liked dashing here and there in his convertible, taking mini-breaks in Europe, visiting obscure castles and hearing their ghost stories. During Frannie's third date with Louis, he got down on one knee and proposed. When she accepted, he ordered champagne for the entire restaurant, toasted her extravagantly, shooed away the lounge pianist and serenaded Frannie himself.

Michael enjoyed seeing Frannie with Louis, who was gentle, charming and utterly impervious to her controlling tendencies. When she shouted, he laughed. When she reminded him of her ironclad plans, he pleaded amnesia. Louis was just the sort of man Frannie needed. He was warm toward everyone, including Michael and James. In fact, for Michael, one of the more surreal moments after the wedding had been sitting at a rose-strewn table with James, Louis and Frannie. James and Louis had fallen deep into conversation and it had been difficult for Michael and Frannie to keep their own discussion on track – Edward's university plans – while watching their respective husbands flirt with one another.

"Hey." James slid his arms around Michael from behind. "Are you going to stare at your manuscript all night?"

"It's ready for upload. If I hit enter, the e-book will be live in forty-eight hours."

"So what are you waiting for? Take Bob's advice. Put it out there."

Michael lifted his face for a kiss. He had no idea where this particular story arose from. The setting – the Greek Isles – came from a vacation he and James had taken two years before. Yet the main character – a grandmother from Manchester – seemed channeled from somewhere unfathomable. Michael suspected he'd never write his own story, not even heavily fictionalized. But somehow while writing about a woman who walked out on her husband, stopped returning her deadbeat son's calls and used her life savings for a one-way trip to a foreign country, Michael felt glimmers of his personal truth come through. After writing and revising the book he'd agonized over highbrow titles – *Nomad*, perhaps, or *Vagabond Life*. Neither seemed right and it was James who suggested the final title, *Granny Does A Runner*.

"Go on," James prodded. "It's perfect."

It wasn't, as Michael very well knew. But James, who would probably never read extensively for pleasure, devoured everything Michael wrote. Each time he finished reading a new piece, James gave his sincere, honest opinion – it was flawless.

Smiling, Michael lifted James's hand to his lips. There were over a hundred places he could go to drum up serious literary criticism. It was nice to have a fan at home.

"Fuck it," Michael grinned, and hit enter.

THE END

Acknowledgements

The author would like to thank the talented and remarkably kind Rebecca Emin for her assistance with the second edition. All correct references to modern English life belong to her. All errors, alas, are mine. Check out Rebecca's blog and her novels here: ramblingsofarustywriter.blogspot.com

About the Author

Orphaned at birth, T. Baggins was raised by wolves until age fourteen, when the pack moved on one night without a forwarding address. Returning to human society, Ms. Baggins taught herself to read and write by studying fan fiction. Cutting her teeth on Kirk/Spock (*Star Trek: The Original Series*, baby!) she soon began slashing rock stars and X-Men. Despite a lifetime spent in the southern U.S., T. Baggins considers herself a citizen of the cosmos and a freethinker, which is good, because no one has offered so much as a penny for her thoughts. In her spare time she enjoys blogging at Shades of Gay, emptying gin bottles and tweeting into the void as @therealtbaggins.

Also by the Author

Fifteen Shades of Gay (For Pay)

Protection

Printed in Great Britain
by Amazon